Wooden Hunters

Wooden Hunters

Matt Cohen

McCLELLAND AND STEWART LIMITED

ISBN 0-7710-2202-6

McClelland and Stewart Limited
The Canadian Publishers
25 Hollinger Road, Toronto

The author would like to acknowledge the assistance of the Canada Council during the writing of this book.

Excerpts from chapter six first appeared in different form in *The Canadian Fiction Magazine* and, under the title "Loose Change," in *The Story So Far/3*.

Printed and bound in Canada
by
John Deyell Company

One

Laurel Hobson was sitting facing into the morning sun, her back supported by water-stained upholstered cushions that came from some now derelict chair that must have been left on the mainland, her feet stretched out into the lake, propped up on a giant grey-weathered cedar log that ran sixty feet straight out from the shore, supporting not only her legs but also the assorted dishes and utensils they have been using, her current cup of coffee and a new bottle of rye, some rosehips spread out to dry for tea and finally Calvin's running shoes, socks and jeans, still wet from last night's hunt and flattened down now onto the log, blood caked onto the dry patches of denim and canvas.

In the evening they had lain under her sleeping bag and watched the sky change colours in the absence of the sun. In that half light small bats swooped and faltered, carving erratic paths, brushing curiously close, one whistling through Calvin's hair in some strange animal current that seemed as ordinary to the place as anything else, as her body absently seeking his while she drank rye out of a plastic cup, as the noises they made that grew so loud Calvin forgot to worry about the rustlings in the bushes, the

1

sounds of the mice and squirrels which had been moving so cautiously in search of the remains of supper and now dashed over the bed in direct attack, their weight skittering across the backs of his thighs like small electric chains.

The sky was dark and when they were disengaged and lying on their backs Calvin could look up and see the stars, the little dipper swinging from the north pole and tipped down into the lake. Laurel Hobson was smoking a cigarette and drinking out of her plastic cup again. They sat up in the bed, the way they had sat in the city, perpendicular to each other with legs tangled together for warmth and their backs curved forward. There had been the first night in Vancouver, one night at her friend's; still they didn't know each other very well, had not touched or wanted to when they were crossing the straits in the ferry, had not touched or wanted to when it was still light and there were all the minimal chores to be done. And when they came together it seemed to him it was out of their bodies' need for it, because it was available, but not badly or only half-there but more than that, maybe better, as if Laurel Hobson had already been turned wild by this island and was imparting the same thing to him, not as a favour but as something he would need to survive.

With the lantern lit they made more coffee and ate the remains of supper. Then the lantern was off and Laurel shone the flashlight across the lake. Two pairs of golden eyes, set narrow, pairs of eyes moving like cats across the opposite shore. "The deer come down there to drink," Laurel Hobson said. He had swum across earlier in the afternoon and seen the tracks, small cloven-hoofed tracks, smaller than dogs' paws or even the hieroglyphs of seagulls.

They seemed to be strangers still and once he had said, as if the frantic noises and accumulated sweat demanded some verbal recognition, "Well, all I feel with you is mindless. I try to think about it but I can't."

2

And she had said something about feeling the same way, whatever that was, no way at all. But now she was smoking her third cigarette in a row and spiking her coffee with the remains of the rye so it seemed, finally, she was working her way up to something and he was wondering what he would do when she came out with the inevitable, which would be that she wanted to keep doing this, living together, recognize whatever this bond was. "Sex is like a drug," Laurel Hobson said. "You get addicted to it." She had gotten the rifle from the end of the bed and had started to take it apart. There was something wrong with the ejection mechanism: when she pulled the bolt back the cartridges would jam up at an angle, or only come out feebly.

"Well," Calvin said, "it doesn't matter; we can fix it in the morning."

"Screw the morning," Laurel Hobson said, standing up now, still naked in the cold night air and slamming the bolt repeatedly, trying to force it into working. "We'll row out in the boat to shoot it," she said. "They stay still for as long as you shine the light at them." She had given up on the bolt and was taping the flashlight to the barrel of the rifle.

All afternoon the lake had been choppy, whipped up by the wind that swept down its narrow length, that seemed to have been brought on by the sun and lingered into the twilight. But now the water was dead calm. From the centre of the lake they could see the moon, barely pushed up past the horizon of the cedar forest: not a full moon, but nearly round with a bite taken out of it. Calvin was rowing the boat slowly, trying not to splash the oars, rowing slowly and nervous too because Laurel was sitting in the back of the boat, the rifle crossed over her knee, staring past him to the shore as if she would just hex the deer to the water, make it go down on its knees and evil it to death.

"Here," she said suddenly, handing Calvin the rifle while he was still rowing, ".you shoot."

"No, that's all right. You go ahead."

She raised the rifle and pressed on the light. The beam was a long narrow cone, bisecting his head and shoulders, travelling straight to the shore. He turned to look, to see if there were any deer, conscious as he turned of the light on his back, of the way they had slept together the first night, not touching, only shifting their bodies into each other in the morning, as if for form's sake. There was a click as the safety went off. He rowed with one oar only, gradually turning the boat.

"No," she said. "Closer. Much closer." He began rowing again, two hands, his head half-turned to aim the boat towards the point where the light touched the shore. He could hear the reeds as they brushed past, bright green reeds that had been cold against his arms and legs when he had swum the lake in the afternoon. There was a sudden jolt as the bow hit a deadhead. The boat rocked.

"Put the safety on," Calvin whispered.

"Don't be dumb." Laurel Hobson swept the shore with the light. Then they saw them again, two pairs of golden eyes. The deer had moved down the shore, were about twenty yards away. "Closer," she said. They moved slowly towards them and as they moved it seemed the deer were drawn to them, to the lamp. It was impossible to see anything of them but their eyes, impossible to tell which one was bigger because the relative heights kept shifting. It was late August, a time of year when the does would still be with their fawns. There would be no bucks, she had explained. They were all in the mountains now, feeding up and getting ready to breed again. "Closer." They hit another deadhead. "Damn," she said loudly. The deer looked up. They were almost on top of them now, maybe ten yards away, and outlines of their bodies were visible in the beam of the flashlight; and although the approach had made the deer wary and their feet were moving nervously they were still held fast by the light which, now, was moving slowly, being raised and centered on the head of the doe, centering and then holding still so that for a moment the light was a taut cable between the eyes and the rifle. And then as the tension began, of itself, and of his own fatigue from travelling to a new city and then coming to this island with Laurel Hobson, who now seemed about to lower her rifle, as the tension began to ebb and settle into some peace so he could be connected to her and to the deer by this light in some mystical or at least final moment that would end and allow each of them to resume where they had left off before this unnecessary melodrama had begun, at the very end of the moment when it was no longer possible for anything to happen there was the explosion of the rifle, a .303 calibre explosion that sent the light swinging wildly up in the air and sound echoing back and forth, from wall to wall turning the lake into a narrow sound chamber, the mountain ridges of cedar forest that rose on either side of it sending the sound back and forth, keeping up a long continuous tone that was periodically slapped by more distant echoes. And then the light was lowered again, following the deer's eyes as they slumped downwards, eyes that were golden now falling apart in colour, going red and green and back to gold again, changing colour wildly like something gone out of control, no peace in this death and in fact it was not dead, Calvin could feel the life still in it, crazy with pain, sending out vibrations back along the beam of light, vibrations that overwhelmed the light and made the rifle tremble, shake with tiny motions in his hands, as he held it, still pointed direct at its eyes, held it because she had handed it to him so she could push closer in towards the shore, towards the deer that now lay stiff on its side but was still sending out its waves of life even when he was standing above it, pointing

5

the rifle and the light at its belly so Laurel Hobson could kneel down by the deer and open its belly to take out the guts and the lungs, holding the heart out to him in her hand, tearing a bite from it and putting it in her pocket; and he could still feel the waves as he shouldered the deer to carry it to the boat, its blood running warm down his neck and shoulders, the weight warm and alive against his back sliding down and into his muscles, towards the water which was seeping into his shoes and pants as he waded out to the back of the boat, thinking he would dump the deer in the passenger seat, still alive; but when he climbed into the boat now entirely soaked with blood and water he still had the deer across his shoulders in the same way, as if it had grown there, as if he was going to have to hold it until it died, the way someone he knew had once come across a car accident and had stepped off the highway and found a young boy trapped inside his car, bleeding and dying, and she had waited with him for the ambulance, waited with him holding his hand and, later she said, glad he died before they came and hurt him more by trying to pry him out; and with the deer across his shoulders he sat in the back of the boat and stared hopefully at the moon as she rowed across the lake. But the moon had nothing to say to him, was only an imperfect white globe, cold rock and dust that pulled the oceans back and forth and reflected the sun's light.

Laurel Hobson led him with the light to a tree and pointed to a spot on the ground. He stood above it and couldn't even figure out how to get this animal, still alive and warm and pliable, off his shoulders and onto the ground. She left him there, standing, in the pitch-black shadows of a grove of scrub alder and cedar, then came back with a saw and the light—finally untaped from the rifle—and a length of yellow nylon rope. She helped him get the animal down and now it was lying on its side, its four feet pointed towards him, dainty cloven hoofs just like the ones that had left tracks by the water last night, dainty feet with white fur. With the saw Laurel Hobson cut the lower half of the two back legs off and then, with her knife, slit the skin at the new breaks and pulled it up so the two bones of the leg were exposed, two bones and the bone which connected them so there was a place to shove through a thick branch she had found. And then looping the yellow nylon rope over a limb of one of the trees Laurel Hobson tied it to the branch that was passed through the deer. Calvin pulled it up, hoisting the deer high into the air, pulled it up until its head was free of the ground; and when she had sawn off the head he pulled it up a little higher. It was easy, the deer was live weight and sending out waves of warmth and blood, it weighed no more than a sack of cement, a young doe who had had her first fawn that spring and now was so much headless meat and fur.

She had brought the lamp to the clearing and now she lit it so they wouldn't have to use the flashlight. She had the bottle too, took some of it and passed it to him. His feet were cold from the water and his shoulders from the absence of the body. He drank the rye but it didn't taste like anything, only hot, drank some more and spat it out.

There was a fallen cedar log a few feet away from the deer and on the log she had placed the lantern and the bottle. Now they both sat down, one on either side of these, him to reach for the bottle again and her to take out a stone from her pocket and begin sharpening her knife. She moved the stone over the steel in slow deliberate circles, not looking at what she was doing but squinting and staring at the deer as if this was to be the contest: Laurel Hobson plus her lamp and her knife versus the doe minus its head and its entrails and a half of each of its hind legs.

When the knife was ready she stepped up to the deer with a look of anticipation, nervous and almost smiling, looking in fact the exact same way she had looked the first night when they were undressing, her eyes round and bright, her mouth broken and open as she lifted her knife to the animal, waves of life still in the air so he could feel it living in him, raised the knife and cut the skin from its front legs first; and then began working the skin free from the top, slitting and pulling it down as she went. It came off like a suit of sticky long underwear, the inside red and shiny with blood.   o

Periodically she would stop and come over to the log for the bottle. Her hands and arms were wet and slippery. When she handed the bottle to him it was slippery too.

"It's sticking," she said. "It shouldn't be sticking like this so soon." And then he had to help her, pulling the skin down over the body, the deer now much colder than when he had carried it, colder and stiff too. Finally they had the skin down to its neck and its front feet and it had changed from the soft, supple fur of a young doe to a problem; they were down on their knees below the animal, on their knees digging their nails into the skin for purchase and pulling, feeling the pressure against their hands and listening to the high-pitched sounds of fibres ripping free.

When Calvin pushed the new hide into the lake the water was warm, warmer than he had expected, warmer than his still-soaked shoes and feet, warm and almost stagnant; and as he washed it, working sand against the places where the flesh and muscle had stuck, he thought he could smell algae and rotting fish from the marsh near where the deer came down to drink. Calvin had the flashlight with him, had put it on the log tilting down into the water so he could see what he was doing. Now he swung it up again, flashed it across the lake, scanning the opposite shore for signs of more deer. "If you want you could make something out of it," Laurel Hobson had said to him while he was carrying the skin down to the lake.

Once, when he was hunting, when he still lived in his

first house, he had found a dead bird. He didn't know what kind it was, but it seemed big. He took his pocketknife and cut off one wing to take home. His parents had bought him a desk then, it was the year he had started to go to school, so in the top drawer along with the pencils and erasers which he never used he kept the wing. It was in the fall and on Saturdays all of those in his neighbourhood who were male and under ten would load up their pockets with stones and go have a war with their richer counterparts who lived across a park and on the other side of the hydro station. He always carried the wing then, on those expeditions, carried it as a necklace, secured inside his sweater with a piece of string. He didn't remember when he had lost it but he still had it when they moved. It smelled strange but never really rotted. Laurel Hobson's offer was unnecessary. Even in memory the wing was too big and too smelly; in his pocket he carried something easy, a fossil of a butterfly that looked like a clam.

Without the skin the deer seemed even more alive. The surface was now an intricate network of grey-blue muscles, sheets of muscle connecting bones and other muscles, nothing wasted, looking as it hung stripped this way absolutely perfect, something that could be admired but not eaten. "Christ," Calvin said, "if a person was skinned and hung up they'd look ridiculous beside that deer."

"You should see a bear," Laurel Hobson said. "Without the head and the fur it looks exactly like a man." The rye was finished and she was sitting on the log, smoking a cigarette.

He was dreaming he was walking down a long silver tunnel and at the end he could see the round silver-grey light from the beach. First it was too bright. He shaded his eyes, squinted into the grey and silver dream and saw that Laurel was at the end of the tunnel. She was walking towards him,

9

smiling, understanding something, her hips swaying so that her skirt moved like a scythe. He woke up and knew that he was dreaming. He could still see her moving towards him. He sat up in the sleeping bag and opened his eyes. The deer was close, closer than it had seemed at night. It was still hanging from the tree, turning slowly in the wind, its ribs swinging in and out of his line of vision, turning slowly in the wind and in the smoke of the small fire beneath it.

He got up out of the sleeping bag and squatted in front of the coleman stove, turning up the flame under the coffee. The morning air was cold against his skin but not as cold as it had been the previous morning. Soon he would feel nothing, his blood would get thinner and rise and fall with the temperature. The sun was visible now, glimmering over the ridge of cedar trees. The deer's muscles still stretched in grey-blue sheets; it was still alive, he could still feel its waves in the air. On the stove, beside the coffee, was a frying pan filled with slices of heart and liver. "You get a deer," Laurel Hobson said, "and then you have to eat it before it goes bad. You eat so much of it that your gut begins to bulge with undigested meat and you shit four times a day."

Laurel Hobson was sitting facing into the morning sun. Calvin went down to the lake with his coffee and then, wanting to swim before he drank it, and rinse off the blood that was still caked onto his shoulders and the back of his neck, stepped around her on the log, over the dishes from last night's supper and over his socks and shoes which she had spread out on the log to dry. The sun pierced easily through the water, illuminating it in long yellow rays. He dove in and swam towards the bottom, the sun through the water making him look yellow-green, long and pale, an unlikely fish with no scales or fins. There were small coloured stones mixed with the sand and mud at the bottom.

He started collecting them, smooth coloured stones that he set one by one on the log, thinking he would make a necklace for Laurel Hobson, something to give her instead of the usual strings of words. When he got back onto the log for his coffee she had brought the pot down to the lake, was re-filling her own cup and spiking it with rye from a newly opened bottle. The bottle was held out towards him. A column of smoke rose from where the deer was hanging. "The flies will get to it soon," she said. "We'll have to finish with it today."

He wondered what the rules were here, whether it was considered normal to hunt and kill animals, and then take them apart. She pointed to a place on her back and asked him to rub it. He had one foot on the log and the other on the spot she had indicated, a vertebra that had been broken and was now permanently swollen, big enough to grind into his foot as he pushed back and forth. Her back was hard and muscular, her spine straight except for the one enlarged bone. "You'd look respectable skinned," he said.

"The first deer is always bad." She turned to look at him, her cigarette in one hand and, in the other, the perpetual cup of coffee with rye.

"Sure," he said, and going back up to the deer saw it turning still, caressed by the smoke of the cedar fire, long dead, dead since the moment he first saw it across the lake.

Two

It seemed that it was always raining on this island, that every morning was equally dull and grey. But even before he opened his eyes Calvin knew that it would be clear. He sat up in the sleeping bag and the first thing he saw was the window, brilliant blue rectangles framed by yellow strips of wood. In this light everything looked different: the new stovepipe shining blue-black, like comic book hair, and near it, hanging from the ceiling, the remaining ribs of the deer, smoked brown and tough, six weeks old, nothing left but bone and gristle.

He had been dreaming, the same dream about Laurel that he always had now. In the dream he was walking down a long silver tunnel, towards her, her silhouette visible against the round silver-grey light from the beach. But this time as he got closer the light intensified, blotted out everything until he emerged into a big open room without walls. Laurel was there, her arms and hands stained with blood from the deer and paint. She was holding out a picture for him to see, a portrait of him that she had done. It was a large rectangular painting of a brick wall, each brick carefully and realistically rendered so that the roughness of the surface could be almost felt. In the top left hand corner was a thick glass window that bulged out, a giant reptilian eye so thick that it was barely transparent. And behind the eye he was posing, looking through like a resigned prisoner, his hands in his pockets and his features calm and blurred.

Later, with the sun higher and warmer, it would be possible to work on the truck. Calvin stood outside, watching the coffee steam into the cold air. As always Laurel had woken up before him, left the cabin hours ago. It was six weeks since she had shot the deer, September now, and the mornings were turning frozen and tight.

Calvin balanced the cup of coffee on the fender of the truck—a broken red International pick-up truck that had come with the cabin. The owner was a loud red-faced man Calvin had met only once, at the grocery store in town. He was the doctor at the island's clinic, and his wife was the nurse. In the store he had looked more like a fisherman than a doctor, his hands awkward and weathered, his manner rough and approximate. His wife was with him in the store. She was tiny, short and thin, and so overwhelmed by him it seemed it must have been their marriage that had reduced her.

The doctor had claimed that the truck had worked, even recently, that there couldn't be much wrong with it. Laurel had nodded in agreement. "He's good at fixing things," she lied to the doctor. "We'll drive in and see you some day soon." Now Calvin put his hands in his pockets, stepped back from the truck and peered at the rusted motor from a distance. He felt suddenly caught in the attitude that Laurel had painted in his dream: Mr. Calvin, the gentleman of leisure, waiting for the movie to begin.

But when he reached out for his coffee he saw himself differently, not blurred but tall and bony, his limbs long and angular. And remembered how easily he had been able to swing the deer into the air, settle it across his back.

With his coffee in his hand, Calvin began to walk

towards the sea. The alder silhouetted against the blue sky, the coloured leaves and frozen morning reminded him of the east but the wetness and fertility of this island, the newness of the air, the speed with which things seemed to grow and then be re-absorbed into the forest floor all made the east seem used and impossible to him, a place that could no longer renew itself, and now sometimes he imagined that whole section of the continent as a vast conglomerate city of doomed smokestacks and concrete.

The morning was clear and still, slowing the ocean and dimming its sounds. Laurel had pinned charts up on the wall and he was learning to know the tides. Between the cabin and the sea were rolling sand dunes with sparse long grass. Calvin crossed the dunes and in the full sun it was already warm. The tide would be coming in now, and with it, the salmon.

He took off his shoes and his shirt, put them on a log high up on the shore, then began to run, his feet slapping into the wet sand at the water's edge. The sun was behind him and he could see his shadow thrown long and skinny, elongated by the morning: and he let his arms go loose so he could watch the black lines jumping across the sand and water. With each step his feet sank into the wet sand, splashed water up onto his pants, making the cuffs flap against his shins. He stopped to roll them up and as he bent down he met the reflection of his face, blurred, the bright sky and sea washing out everything but his eyes.

The stream wound into the sea from between sand cliffs. At low tide its mouth was warm and shallow, only a few inches deep, separated from the sea by long narrow sandbars that were re-formed with each tide. Even then the salmon would sometimes try to struggle across, flopping on the hot narrow sand until they were swallowed by the stream, resting for a moment in the shallow freshwater before moving up, searching for deeper, cooler places. But the best time to catch them was as the tide came in. Then they flowed from the ocean into the stream in thick clusters. Laurel had already set the net and was upstream from it, her head bent down and her arms and hair layered in great white clouds of foam and soap. Beside the stream was the table they used for filleting the fish. And, behind that, the smokehouse the doctor had built. Calvin sat on the table, ran his hands over the smooth handsplit cedar. Now it was clean, but soon it would be stained with blood and eggs. The land back from the beach had once been logged. They were more careless then—many of the trees that still stood were hundreds of years old, fir and cedar that rose into the sky like masts for some ship too big to even imagine. And of the trees that had been felled but were left rotting on the ground, many were still sound, red cedar ten feet across at the base. With a chainsaw and axes they prepared wood for the smokehouse.

"And," Laurel had said, "when you've fixed the truck we can drive up here and bring the wood back to the cabin." As if, having provided him, a stranger and a visitor, with the sea and the forest, it was only reasonable to expect he could supply the rest, could revive this truck that had been drowned by the tide while the doctor drank wine and dreamed about the vagaries of life in the hands of nature.

His feet were only halfway adapted from the city and running made them tender and sore, grateful for the cool wet grass along the bank of the stream. At least one fish was trapped in the net, struggling vigorously, its tail splashing through the surface of the water, gradually creating mounds of foam on each of the small plastic floats. There was no alder here, only spruce and fir and cedar. The sun came through the trees in long misty shafts, transforming the forest into a ridiculously beautiful apparition, a vast kaleidoscopic cathedral of shifting lights and colours, turning his body inside out to the end of summer.

Later, when it seemed that the morning was over, and the shadows and coolness had both given way to pure heat, Laurel went back to the cabin. Calvin stayed out, on the beach, walking up and down as he did every afternoon. Sometimes he felt like a scientist on a new planet, and spent the time inspecting all the strange tiny flowers and stones, poking the barnacles on rocks to watch them open and close, trying to memorize the strange shapes and colourations of the shore birds and the high sand cliffs that lined the beach.

But this day was too hot for concentration. Even walking with Laurel part way down on the beach, the sun had dazed him, crept comfortably into his bones and made him feel so lazy he just returned to the stream and sat in the shade of a huge old cedar tree that was rooted into the bank.

The stream changed sizes with the tide. As it got smaller it revealed the stones that enclosed it. Once his foot hit a sharp point and moved involuntarily. It landed on sand and as he let it take his weight he noticed something else, smooth and cold against his instep. He reached down and picked up the stone his foot had touched. It was wet and ochre-coloured, shaped into an oval. Its surface was smooth. The red was broken by strange white streaks. He put the stone in his pocket and climbed up onto the bank again. This stream emptied the lake into the ocean, the lake where they had killed the deer. Its water was tinged with red, rust-coloured bearing traces of iron and copper.

He sat on the bank, staring at the stream. It moved with amazing speed, its centre cut deep by the water. Somehow it made him doze. Even though his eyes stayed open he could feel and see the morning again, playing back like a slow dance in his mind. And in his belly too, which was open and clean, the tension temporarily broken and drained by Laurel and by the day so each breath seemed to go deeper into him, so much more oxygen that he felt like he was floating.

He took off his clothes and stepped slowly into the water. In the morning Laurel had pushed him in but now he went carefully, splashing himself first to break the cold. Then let the stream carry him down towards the ocean before he started fighting his way back, kicking and splashing furiously, waking himself up.

When he went back he could hear voices as he approached the cabin. Johnny Tulip would be there, sitting inside, talking and drinking with Laurel. Calvin stopped, considered turning back, then went inside anyway, too hungry to do anything else.

Johnny Tulip was slouched back in his chair, a bottle of wine settled comfortably in his hand. He jumped up when Calvin came in, bowed and swept out his free arm in welcome. He was a short thick man with a face so big it seemed to explode from his head. His skin was dark and weathered, covered his features like a careless hide, battered, creased and scarred past what any of his stories could tell.

"My good man," Johnny Tulip said. He grinned at Calvin, a wide grin that split his huge face in halves. His voice was like nothing Calvin had ever heard, a big old motor about to give up, honeycombed by decades of smoking and drinking.

"Did you see any seals?" Laurel asked. Her face was flushed from the wine.

Calvin shook his head. He drew up a chair and Johnny sat back down. "You must have seen a seal," Johnny Tulip said. He leaned forward. His eyes were deep brown, sunk deep into his skull, enfolded in dark skin so always, whether he was drunk, or talking nonsense, or trying to push him into something, Calvin found them opaque and impenetrable. Johnny took a deep breath. It rattled through his chest. He leaned even closer to Calvin. "The seals see you," he said. "You can't go anywhere without the seals seeing you." His voice ground in on itself. Stopped and waited, what for Calvin never knew, alternately attracted and repelled by this strange man who seemed impossible to respond to, who periodically inserted himself between Calvin and Laurel in what seemed to be a long and hopeless attempt to find new ways to pass the time.

"What about Vancouver?" Laurel finally asked. "Can the seals follow you all the way to Vancouver?" She winked at Calvin.

"Fly to Vancouver in a big silver bird," Johnny Tulip said hoarsely. He waved his arms like a cigar store Indian in full flight. "Go downtown and buy a guitar. Be a star." He slapped his big hands on the table and leaned forward again to Calvin. "Do you want to be a star?"

Laurel laughed. Her shirt was partly unbuttoned, showing her throat and the tops of her breasts, flushed too, and Calvin could feel the jealousy coming alive in his stomach and chest, the morning swept away by the idea of Johnny Tulip here all afternoon, drinking and laughing with her while he was out in the impossibly hot sun, hunting invisible seals.

"He is a star," Laurel said. "He rose up out of the east and now he's here."

"Me too," Johnny Tulip said. "I rose up out of my mother and now I'm here." When he laughed his voice broke apart entirely, avalanching into his lungs and turning into long dry coughs.

Laurel looked with concern at Johnny, then winked again at Calvin. "We fixed the truck," she said. "Tonight we can go to hear Johnny play at the bar. He spent all yesterday trying to tune the piano."

18

Calvin inspected the counter, trying to see if there was anything easy to eat. Johnny Tulip had finally stopped coughing, was taking a sip of the wine. "All right," Calvin said. "That would be nice." He looked at Johnny Tulip's hands. They were still on the table, spread flat with the fingers splayed wide apart. The backs of his hands were wide and corrugated with broken knuckles and blue veins that rose up out of his skin like mountains. His fingers were long and thin, but twisted and bent in unpredictable directions.

"They don't look too good now, do they?"

"Well," Calvin said. "They have character." He spread his own hands out on the table. On the back of his left hand was tattooed a blue and green anchor. Otherwise his hands looked like they always had, unused, unchanging from year to year except for the pores which seemed to be gradually developing individual terrains.

"A tattoo," Johnny Tulip said. "You must be a sailor."

"Oh no," Calvin said. "All stars have tattoos." The first night he was with Laurel she had noticed it too, had poured rye on it and rubbed it as if it was impossible that it be real.

"My father was a sailor," Johnny Tulip said. "He used to help paddle the missionaries back and forth from the mainland. Then he signed up on a ship that went down to the Panama Canal and around the other side."

"What happened?"

"He came back," Johnny Tulip said. "He was gone for four years, and my mother was living with someone else, an old man who would never tell anyone his name." He cleared his throat and coughed.

"His name was Johnny Tulip too," Laurel said. "Johnny Tulip's real father's name was Harry Jones. His mother said she had already married one Harry Jones and he wasn't any good so she wasn't going to have any more of

19

them around the house. When she took the old man in she called all the children after him."

Johnny Tulip laughed his crazy broken laugh, laughed and then coughed again. It seemed impossible to Calvin that this man could have a past, at least a past other than what he carried with him, marked into his body and face, so much his own now that other people's mistakes could no longer touch him. And now as his coughs subsided and Johnny Tulip looked across the table at him, Calvin was swept by a sudden flash of nervousness, a recognition of his own insubstantial and alien spirit, as it must seem to Johnny Tulip, a spirit so fragile and so white it could only stagger in and out of the cabin, Mr Calvin, the gentleman of leisure, like a weak but persistent moth waiting to be burned.

In the centre of the table Johnny had placed the now-empty bottle of cheap red wine, Calona red, the kind he always brought with him when he came to visit Laurel. If he brought one bottle Laurel would drink it with him. She would also drink with him, to the end of every bottle, if he brought three or four.

"Johnny's mother is blind," Laurel said. "She never minds how anyone looks. Which is just as well."

"My mother loves me," Johnny said. "She has the second sight." Again his face split into halves with his grin, his jaw and lower cheeks smooth and wide, the upper part of his face solemn and unchanged. Calvin tried to imagine what Johnny's mother would look like blind. Perhaps like Johnny, with hollow eyes.

"She can tell the future," Laurel said. "But she won't." And then, as if she had been reading Calvin's mind, added, "She never opens her eyes either. But she has the most beautiful lashes."

Laurel got out of her chair to inspect the empty bottle. She was so pink from the wine that the whites of her eyes seemed even whiter than normal to Calvin, as if the morning and the afternoon had somehow combined to cancel each other out. She had told Calvin she was twenty-five years old but the way she laughed and attacked the bottle she might have been older or younger. It didn't matter, she had taken on the colouration of west coast bars and liquor stores and become one of those people who carries her whole life with her, all of it present at once. And although he found that beautiful and exemplary, making him feel like a suicide in comparison, with his amputated memories and incarnations, it didn't seem to have guaranteed Laurel Hobson anything because he kept seeing her lives go in different directions, so she was constantly tripping and falling over some old pattern that should have been discarded long ago.

Calvin stood up and went out to get water for tea. They had stayed at the lake for two weeks after killing the deer. Then the nights and the mornings started to get colder and Laurel told him about the cabin. "You can come if you want to," she had said.

"All this fresh air," Calvin had said. "It makes me nervous." They were sitting on the log that jutted out into the lake, the long cedar log that still seemed to point accusingly across to the clearing where they had taken the deer. "Or maybe it's you that's making me nervous," Calvin said, immediately annoyed at the sound of his own voice, stupid and coy.

But Laurel didn't even seem to notice, only lit another cigarette and pointed down to the end of the lake, to the stream she told him flowed sluggishly outwards, wound for miles through marsh and forest until it got quicker and deeper, finally emptying in the ocean. The same stream, she said, where they would catch the salmon when they started their run. Like the doctor used to before he got

21

married, deserting his clinic for two weeks every fall, performing all his operations with a gaff hook and a filleting knife.

Sometimes she cried but it always seemed without reason, at night when they were ready to go to sleep. She would burrow into him, her arms trapped between their chests, and her face pressed against his neck, crying without noise or movement. Just tears. She had stopped drinking though, after the deer, nothing at all until they moved down to the cabin and started going to town some nights.

They got their water from a clearing a hundred yards away from the cabin. There was a well, a twenty-foot well that was hand-dug and lined with large round stones from another place on the island, where it was flatter and rockier, and fields had been ploughed by the original white settlers. The well had been built to serve a house. But the house had burnt down long ago; the only sign of its existence was a shallow square depression in the ground where the grass grew slightly faster and greener. When Laurel had first shown him the old well it was covered by a piece of plywood that was quickly rotting away. Now they had put up four posts and a roof of split shakes to protect the well: so coming upon it from the path with the shakes still red and un-weathered it looked impossibly new, and useless, a red cedar roof stuck up in the air, just high enough so they could get under it and, using the yellow nylon rope, now tied from the crossbar, throw the bucket down into the water.

When he got back to the cabin Laurel had cleared the table of the wine and the glasses, had set out the teapot and plates, was standing at the coleman stove adjusting the lid over the frying salmon steaks, butter and fat from the fish sputtering noisily against the metal, like popcorn.

Johnny Tulip was outside somewhere but there were

three plates on the table. "I think he's being sick," Laurel said, coming to Calvin, putting her arms around him and snaking her hands inside his shirt. Her lips were swollen and bitter with wine.

"I have to have you," she whispered, giggling, pressing against him. Then she pushed back and smiled at him, her eyes hard and bright, and he could see the deer swinging in the smoke of the fire.

Three

The bar was in a new hotel they had built at the north end of the island to accomodate the loggers and the fishermen. The owner of the hotel, an American who had sold his small feed business in Montana and moved to this island, employed himself as the barman. He had a long list of exotic and nearly undrinkable specialties which he served to Indians and whites without discrimination, even giving away the most artistic of his creations to those who were too shy or sensible to buy them.

"Aah shit," he liked to say around closing time, when his cash register was overflowing and the particular day's prospect of order was more or less destroyed. "I guess I made enough money in Great Falls to last me longer than I'll ever live."

In his wallet he carried a small card,

C.W. Smith
Wholesale Grain

and a colour picture of his wife, Gladys. No one knew what his initials stood for. "I got enough to last me," C.W. would say, "but Gladys, my god, a man never had a more expensive wife." In the colour picture it was hard to see exactly what was so expensive about Gladys. It couldn't have been the modest white frame house set in the middle of absolutely flat Montana desert, or even the ordinary-looking car which she was leaning against. Perhaps it was the cat she was holding, a long-haired white Persian cat that was clutched against her chest and obviously trying to scratch her.

C.W. may have paid himself generously for his work as bartender. But Johnny Tulip, best and only piano player within a thousand miles of the mainland, received only a dollar and fifty cents an hour for his efforts—a dollar fifty an hour, plus two bottles of beer.

The waitresses were paid even less. They would work for exactly eight weeks, long enough to draw unemployment insurance. They didn't save anything because after eight weeks in C.W.'s bar they could only fly down to Vancouver and drink until their money was gone.

Of all the waitresses he employed on his yearly cycle, Laurel was C.W.'s absolute exception. It was C.W.'s custom, in the painful absence of his expensive wife, to console himself with his employees. Not in any gross or unforgiveable way after-hours but only while they worked, giving little bonus pats and pinches every time they came behind the bar to deposit empty glasses or fill new orders. The first day Laurel worked there, C.W. bestowed his usual favours. Laurel tried to stare him down. C.W. mistook her glances for encouragement, and persisted. Laurel told him that she had syphilis and couldn't touch strange men. C.W. laughed and patted her. Laurel did nothing. C.W. thought she must have acquiesced and continued as usual. Everything was normal. On the fourth day, C.W. was standing in the middle of the floor, giving forth with some of his closing-time best. As Laurel passed him, C.W. reached out for her. Laurel stopped. She set down her tray on the nearest table and threw her arms around his neck.

"Oh C.W.," Laurel said. "You're too much." She dropped to her knees in front of him and clasped her hands at his belt. "You're just too much." Then she quickly undid his belt and pulled down his grey and black striped trousers and his red flowered boxer shorts. "I brought you a present," Laurel said. She reached into her blouse and pulled out a picture with bits of tape at the edges. She stuck the picture to where his shirt-tail hung down below his vest and between his knees. Then she got up and walked behind the bar. One of the customers came over to her and ordered a drink. Others followed. C.W. stood in the middle of the room, his pants and shorts swirled about his ankles, a picture of a banana pinned to his shirt. People started talking again. C.W. pulled up his pants and tucked in his shirt and his banana. Laurel handed him a tray of mixed drinks and C.W. delivered them about the room. "Last call," C.W. said.

Although C.W. Smith knew the names of his waitresses, he didn't call the hotel anything. He had simply brought a sign up with him from Montana, a red-lettered neon HOTEL that was the only neon sign on the whole island. HOTEL was wreathed with green leaves. Not only did these green leaves flash on and off, with the red letters, but periodically, every six flashes, the light ran round them in green circles, circling twice and then stopping to resume flashing again. Truly an arresting sign and they could see not only its red glow but also the pulsing green before they were even near the hotel, the light from the sign so unusual in the town that it was visible from around the corner, flowing down the main street like an electric river.

They were all three in the front seat of the truck: Calvin driving, Laurel in the middle, and Johnny Tulip on the outside. Johnny Tulip was drinking the second bottle of wine, wearing one of his endless supply of blue serge jackets, a black felt hat and, in his lapel, orange paper flowers that Laurel had made him after supper.

It was Johnny Tulip's forty-seventh birthday. Johnny Tulip had the window open and was waving the bottle at the empty street. During the summer, with tourists and fishing, the population of the town swelled to six hundred. But in the winter it was barely half of that, just enough to support the public school and a new government-subsidized sewer system that was being run up and down all the streets of the town, past what were mostly empty lots and old shacks, past the offices of the logging company and up the hill to where the management lived. There the company had their prefabricated bungalows that had been ferried north from Vancouver and placed in semi-circular dead-end crescents: with bay windows all facing in and the backyards all facing out in a circle, like a wagon train formed up for the attack. Before they went to the hotel they had to tour these crescents, Johnny Tulip waving and shouting out the names of the men he knew from the logging camps while Calvin revved the motor and flashed the headlights on and off.

"It's my birthday tonight," Johnny Tulip said as they pulled the truck up in front of the hotel.

"Tonight you're a star for sure," Laurel said.

"I rose up out of my mother and here I am," Johnny Tulip said. They were passing the bottle back and forth in the front seat.

"Might as well finish this now," Johnny Tulip said.

"Sure," Calvin said. Reaching across Laurel for the bottle. And then, after taking a pull, pushing the lights of the truck off and noticing, when he pushed, that the switch travelled right through the rusted dashboard and landed at his feet.

"It's my birthday tonight," Johnny Tulip said again. He had first announced this after Calvin had come in from the well, declining tea on the grounds that he had decided that for at least one day a year he could destroy the remains of his kidneys and liver, that in fact he now remembered the doctor had said alcohol was better than tea.

From the truck they could hear the bass of the jukebox, a steady pounding that seemed to be independent of any melody or even other instruments. But when they went inside even that was lost in the turbulence of voices and lights. Only C.W. could be heard above it all, standing in the middle of the room, a round plastic tray of drinks held above his shoulders, Montana specials that he had started to give away because although it was nine o'clock, it was Saturday night and he had been drinking since early in the afternoon.

"Johnny Tulip," C.W. shouted, wrapped one long arm around Johnny's shoulders and, with the other, offered the tray. The drinks were presented in round plastic goblets, C.W.'s trademark and protection against ingrates. They took on strange colours, in the red and green lights of the lounge, and their olives and cherries were hard to distinguish. Accepting C.W.'s generosity was a hit and miss affair.

"C.W.," Johnny shouted back. "It's my birthday tonight."

"Hey," C.W. shouted. Then he spotted Laurel and Calvin working their way through the crowd. He hesitated. He had never seemed quite carefree in Laurel's presence since the night she pulled down his black and grey striped pants.

But Laurel went straight to him, took a drink off his tray. "How the hell are you?" She had her hand on his arm. Johnny Tulip pulled her so the three of them were enclosed in a triangle.

"Look," Johnny Tulip said. "It's my birthday tonight."
Now that the three of them were turned into each other the

room had picked up again. "No one even remembered," Johnny said. "Not even my mother."

"Mothers never really love you," C.W. said. "If my mother had loved me better, I'd be a better man today."

"That's an awful thing to have to say," Johnny Tulip said. He had finished his first drink and helped himself to another.

"It's awful but it's true," C.W. said sadly.

"No," Johnny said. "I can't say I'd say that, no. I rose up out of my mother and here I am. What man can fault the mother who birthed him and fed him from her own very own body?"

"I myself was a bottle baby," C.W. said. "My mother, and of course my father, who founded the Smith feed grain business in Great Falls, Montana when there were still memories of open ranges and cattlemen had only started to use feed lots to raise beef, would once a week every Sunday mix a week's supply of my formula, milk replacer my father used, said it was good enough, and put it in the old frigidaire which they kept behind the stairs, pre-bottled, so all they had to do was heat it up six times a day."

"A tragic story," Johnny Tulip said. He performed a replacement of his own, coming up with his third straight free special. Standing beside C.W. he appeared to come not only from a different race, but a whole different conception of humanity. C.W. seemed to have been squeezed out of some enigmatic machine, tall and thin with his belly and his face held in tight, his muscles pushing in and pushing out at the same time so the edges of his body exuded a strange static tension, as controlled as his cleanly shaven face, his close-cropped black hair.

Johnny Tulip was shorter and wider. His whole life's disasters were written into the stiff and eccentric ways he moved, his scarred and swollen features. Even his hair had become absolutely unique: it came down straight and dry, like black and silver straw, from the widow's peak that had now receded high up onto his scalp, so the hair sprayed forward on either side of his oversize face.

"They claimed I gained weight very quickly," C.W. said. But now he was tall and thin, like an undertaker in his striped trousers and striped vest, a full head taller than Johnny or Laurel. Then seeing that his tray was rapidly being transformed, he took away Johnny's drink and pulled himself back. "Work tonight," C.W. said.

The piano was a baby grand, old and out of tune. It had been brought to the island on a barge, by the missionary Johnny Tulip's father used to take back and forth from the mainland. After its arrival it had lived in different places, transported first by horses on a wagon, then later by truck, but none of its homes, except for this hotel, had been heated all year round. Its strings had grown thick and rusty, parts of the insides had expanded and contracted too many times. Now Johnny Tulip was the only person who could play it. His tunes were all vaguely familiar, honky-tonk and ragtime tunes from the twenties and thirties. He never sang but sometimes, in the summer, tourists would gather at the piano while he played, put their arms around each other's shoulders and sing the old songs.

While Johnny Tulip played, Calvin listened to Laurel talking. She was telling some story to the others at their table, the doctor who owned the cabin and, of course, now that she had favoured him, C.W., who flipped his string tie between his fingers, adjusted the silver cactus-shaped clip. Calvin had his hands wrapped round his beer and was watching the big vein on the back of his left hand pulse the tattoo in and out. The room seemed uncertain, filled with currents of hostile energy. He wondered if Johnny Tulip would join in the inevitable fight or just keep playing as the place was dismantled.

Whatever it was about her that had been irritating him in the afternoon, that awareness she had of herself and her independence that sometimes seemed ugly to him though he didn't know why, was bothering him now. And while Laurel was talking Calvin found himself drinking more quickly than he had in years, several beers in quick succession, feeling not a desire to get drunk but only a thirst that seemed to stretch right through his body, as if there was some actual deficiency the beer would fill. Half of his attention was focused on C.W., Johnny Tulip at the piano, Laurel and her landlord; the other half followed the waitress around the room nervously. Tonight it was Mary Gail who was working. Johnny Tulip's sister, she was less than half Johnny's age and her face was as smooth and expressionless as Johnny's was broken and volatile. It was only after he persuaded her to leave four glasses in front of him that he took his eyes off her at all. Then he let himself lean forward over the table, close his eyes and wrap his hands around the glass, cool and wet, his mind sliding back to the last time he had drunk so much. "I used to buy a case of twenty-four and take it to parties, sit on it all night until it was empty," was what he almost said to Laurel, when she turned to him, obviously surprised at the sudden accumulation of glasses. But instead he said nothing, saw only himself the last few months in the city, every night the same, sitting in the apartment with a quart of rye in front of him which he would drink until half-way into the morning, drinking and reading and listening to the rantings of the all-night disc jockey. Then, noticing Laurel was looking at him curiously, Calvin wanted to say something about how remarkable it was he could sit with his eyes open, pointing at her, yet not see her face but some image out of the past. But it didn't hold, began to be replaced by a recognizably beer-like mist.

"Are you all right?"

"Of course," Calvin said, her question making him count the remaining full glasses, one, so he turned and looked for Mary Gail again. His stomach felt pushed out and swollen. He burped and leaned forward, putting his hand on Laurel's as Mary Gail came by. Laurel's skin was brown and firm, stretched tightly over the bones and muscles. Naked she looked like a hybrid of human and cat, her flesh dispensed in perfect proportions of muscle and fat, she seemed to move on a principle of balance known only to herself, as if her kind of cat was made up entirely of secrets, not like Mary Gail whose arm, as it brushed his shoulder, seemed softer and almost vulnerable, and turning to inspect her face he was relieved to see her skin was imperfect too, mottled with the heat and noise of the bar, copper splotched with pink, speaking of alcoholic nights surely followed by unspeakable days. Johnny Tulip was now moving into jazzed up versions of old Broadway songs and Calvin found himself tapping his foot, humming under his breath, noticed only when Laurel moved that he had been keeping time on her instep.

"Are you sure you're all right?"

"Of course." Mary Gail had seen what he needed, and left four more glasses of draft in front of him. He pushed one over to Laurel, watching the trail of the glass through the wet film of beer that covered the table. She was looking at him the way she always did when he was about to do something she didn't like, wide brown eyes pointed blankly at him, asking if he really wanted this. Despite everything that was animal about her she always seemed entirely rational to him, each action thought out and consecutive, one day following the other in some great inevitable framework whose shape was known to her, if no one else, its existence guaranteed by the absolute conviction with which she did everything—from the time he had first met her when she was methodically going through the bottle of rye, and him, to the way she had brought him up here and moved him from the lake to the cabin, to now, when, he didn't know why, he could feel his thought patterns breaking apart under the impetus of the beer moving from his stomach to his blood, charging through his body in great uneven swoops, percolating into his bones, the marrow. When they had dissected a cat in zoology he had noticed the marrow was yellow, an irresolute cross between beer and earwax.

He couldn't help himself, wanted to do something really unforgiveable in answer to this innocent look she was giving him, say something that would make her lose her composure for once, throw a glass of beer in her face. The memory of the morning pushed itself through. They had gone swimming in the stream and then made love. Lying in the cold grass, wet, the trapped salmon splashing and fighting, killing itself by its own struggle. Laurel's thighs cold and wet, slippery like a fish too, soundless, he wondered if she thought herself one of the ones that had made it upstream, if she would be taking a child from him as casually as anything else. Then she had pulled him in deeper, everything suddenly sucked out of him and he was empty, riding into her hollow as the tide roaring into the beach. But when they were finished and standing, still dripping, he noticed that the net had stopped moving and without pause Laurel walked from him to the net, pulled it in and took out the salmon, twenty-five pounds and just turning pink on its stomach, laid it on the table and opened it up quickly, not squeamishly the way he had been with the cat but in a practised ritual, pulling out the guts and eggs and pushing them off the table, turning to him as if there was nothing left to say, then walking towards him, suddenly sliding her hands up onto his chest rubbing in blood and eggs; and he had felt something strange and unexperienced since childhood, a current jumping through his body so forcefully he seemed to have been jolted on his feet, a current of mixed fear and violence that surprised him into grabbing her, hugging her against him so they were both covered with the insides of the salmon, then the current jumped again and was gone, leaving him drained and passive, unresisting while she pushed him down the bank and into the stream where, swimming lazily against the current, he felt again the empty bowl of his stomach and genitals. And when he climbed back up onto the bank Laurel was waiting for him with her shirt held out as a towel, her eyes wide open the way they were now, projecting, he never was quite sure which, understanding or indifference.

"Hey," C.W. shouted. Johnny had his fists closed and was pounding on the keys, stamping his feet and shouting along with the noise from the piano. The Indians in the bar had all stood up and were watching Johnny Tulip. "Hey," C.W. shouted again and somehow, through everything, Johnny heard him, turned his head in his direction and brought up. Calvin was now so drunk that the sudden cessation of noise caught him by surprise, had to travel from somewhere deep in his bones where it had been living to his brain and then out his ear and back again. Johnny had climbed down from the stage and was walking towards Calvin. He had left his black felt hat at the table and now Calvin stood up, ready to hand it to Johnny. He couldn't understand how he had drunk so much beer. He narrowed his eyes, tried to find a place in the centre of his pupils that he could still see through. With his eyes focused and his hand steadying himself at the table he felt in control again, stepped forward to help Johnny. But the table was wider than he remembered, sideswiped his hip and jolted over.

"It's okay Johnny," Calvin said. He had put Johnny's hat on his head, so he wouldn't forget it. He couldn't see Laurel anywhere. "Sometimes a man has to think things over."

Johnny walked right by him, as if he wasn't there, without even taking his hat, heading towards the door. Calvin followed him. Through the door of the lounge and the hall, out into the cold air that was suddenly dark and wet, so cold it caught in his throat and chest, air filled with wind from the sea and red and green light from the HOTEL sign, the leaves now a constant running and blinking blur around the edges of a fuzzy red oval. Calvin coughed and could feel the beer bubbling in his stomach, lining his lungs and all the membranes inside him. Coughed again and then thought he heard Johnny cough, rushed forward to see if he had been sick. He pushed the hat further down on his head so it wouldn't fall off, followed Johnny as he walked quickly and without staggering down the main street, his back illuminated by the ever dimming river of light from the hotel, walking quicker and quicker so finally Calvin had to run to catch up to him.

"Stupid fucking doctors," Johnny said. He stopped suddenly and coughed, clutching his arms across his chest. Nothing came out. Then he spat, red.

Johnny Tulip led him through a maze of streets and alleys, past a warehouse then up a narrow path to the top of a hill. They were overlooking the narrow inlet that gave the town access to the sea. The moon was out and they could see the fishing boats tied up at the small docks. And, just a bit further out, two log barges. "Should know better," Johnny Tulip said. They had found some rocks to sit on and Johnny Tulip had a cigarette in his hand, was trying to find a match.

"Here," Calvin said. He remembered again the man who had given him the tattoo, lighting his cigarette in the alcohol lamp he used for sterilising the needles. Lighting it and then leaving it in his mouth as he worked, the ashes falling off from their own weight, sometimes onto Calvin's arm, or when the man noticed, onto the floor as he shook his head in time with the falling ash. Calvin held out a match to Johnny Tulip, took the cigarette he was offered while trying to light Johnny's, ended up only burning his fingers.

"I'll do it," Johnny Tulip said.

"It's okay," Calvin said. He started to say something else but felt closed out. He lit his own cigarette and then passed the package. The beer was still in him, but no longer at the centre, only something acrid and sour in his body, along for the ride.

"What are you going to do?"

"I don't know," Calvin said.

"A man has a few drinks on his birthday and then he gets sick."

"Oh."

"Here," Johnny Tulip said. He held out his hand. There was a knife in the flat of his palm.

Calvin hesitated.

"Take it," Johnny Tulip said. "Go ahead."

Calvin still hesitated. The feeling he had had at the beginning of the night came back, the inevitability of the fight. "I don't have anything against you," Calvin said.

"Take it," Johnny Tulip said. Calvin couldn't hear anything in his voice. Nerves in his arms and back were exploding. He shifted his weight, could feel his feet sliding forward in his boots. He took the knife, stepped back.

"Thank you," Johnny Tulip said. "A man shouldn't carry a knife when he's drunk."

"Sure," Calvin said. "Best be careful." It was a bone-handled hunting knife. He waited until Johnny looked away and then ran his thumb slowly against the blade. It wasn't very sharp. He slipped the knife into his belt.

"Nervous."

"Yes."

"I always wanted to look good," Johnny Tulip said. "Afraid to get hit in the face." It was hard for Calvin to imagine how Johnny Tulip might have looked twenty years ago. Driving from the cabin to the bar there had been no moon, only late summer stars, barely visible through the glare of the headlights. Now it was so late the winter constellations had started to show, Orion was visible and, just on the horizon, Sirius, swollen and yellowed by the haze of smoke from the logging camps. The moon was up too. Half a moon and in its light Johnny Tulip looked grey and old. Only his eyes and teeth showed in the light of the moon.

"Fucking loggers," Johnny Tulip said.

Calvin nodded. The beer was finding its way into him again. He rocked back and forth as he sat and smoked. He could feel the handle of the knife rubbing against his waist.

"I come up here on my birthday six years ago," Johnny Tulip said. "Me and my brother and two bottles of wine but we were already drunk before we came." He took another cigarette from the package and lit it against the butt of the one he was smoking. "We came up here and it was a night like this, clear." He stood up to grind out his old cigarette, stumbled, then turned away from Calvin.

"The best time to piss is when you're drunk," Johnny Tulip said.

"Yeah," Calvin said. His bladder was full and sharp but somehow he didn't want to move. Finally he did, stretched, and then took a few short steps. His fingers felt dead on his fly, the zipper was too complicated and he considered taking down his pants.

"My brother could piss for three minutes without stopping," Johnny Tulip said.

"I don't have a brother."

"My family used to be famous for how long they could piss," Johnny Tulip said. "When they built the church we used to have contests, every Sunday. My sister Victoria was the best of all; she could go so long her feet got wet."

"Oh."

"She drowned," Johnny Tulip said. "Drowned six

years ago today." Calvin somehow completed his man-
oeuvre and was sitting down again. "They told her she had
some kind of cancer, inside her. She rowed out into the
water about a mile and then jumped in. I found her on the
beach. Fuck. I dropped my cigarette." There was a hissing
sound. Then Johnny was finished. He came and sat down
again, lurching as he lowered himself to the rock, bouncing
off Calvin's shoulder. And beneath the surface of the beer
Calvin's body was starting to come into focus, his belly
bloated and tense, splitting apart with the same current that
had been there in the morning, pushing through his nerves
like a drunken puppeteer making him look over to see if
Laurel was coming up the path, sending his left hand to the
knife and his right to Johnny's shoulder, steadying him,
pushing him away with the thought that he was bigger and
more sober than Johnny Tulip; it would be easy. Then he
caught their common scent of cheap red wine and beer,
some of it already passed through Johnny's stomach and
the supper of rice and beans they had eaten at the cabin.
"My brother used to work in the logging camps," Johnny
Tulip said. "He worked there one, two months, then collected unemployment insurance. But he could never keep a
woman."

"No," Calvin said, hardly hearing Johnny Tulip, the
sound lying dead in his stomach.

"You're too young to know anything." Johnny Tulip
burped and then, falling forward onto his knees, began in
long liquid sighs to bring up everything that remained.
Each time Johnny contracted Calvin's stomach jumped in
sympathy. He turned away and lit a cigarette. "When you're
older, it just hurts more," Johnny said. "It shouldn't be like
that." His voice was hoarse and bubbly, drawn through the
liquid that was still in his throat and chest. He coughed.

"No," Calvin said. Again he was aware of the knife in
his belt, wondered if Johnny Tulip was going to tell him a

horrible story about his brother committing suicide on his birthday, like his sister had, and then ask Calvin to kill him too, so they would all three die on the same day.

"I don't know what I wanted to look good for," Johnny Tulip said. He tore some grass away, chewed it briefly and then spat. In the tattoo parlour Calvin had been afraid to take off his shirt, so he had looked away from the man and offered the only exposed part, the back of his hand and wrist. "Do you believe I looked good?"

"It's sincerity that counts," Calvin said. He felt on the other side of his body now, at least flimsily protected from the pains that were still in his belly and groin.

"Oh yes," Johnny Tulip said. "You know my brother was like that. Never lied. He had a woman but couldn't keep her."

"What happened."

"I ran away with her, we went down to Vancouver and she got a job in a bar and while she worked there I'd come and she'd sneak drinks to me until she got too big to work anymore. The night she was going to have the baby I got drunk and waited in the hospital, and all the time I thought there would be something wrong with it because she was my brother's woman. Then the doctor came out and said everything was all right and when I saw it, it looked exactly like him."

"You must have been happy." He wondered if Johnny could hear his voice echo.

"Sure," Johnny said. "I sent her back to live with him but then she ran away with someone else." He turned towards Calvin, his elbow high in the air as he dragged on his cigarette. And then Johnny Tulip was turning faster, the space between filled with his movement and suddenly Calvin saw that the hand was driving towards his throat. He could feel it before it hit him, Johnny's big broken fingers clamping into him; and one of his own arms was already up

39

to block Johnny Tulip, then moving forward, the hand with the tattoo clenched into a fist. Stopping suddenly at Johnny Tulip's blue serge jacket; stopped by himself but also by Johnny's hand spread out like an iron net, swallowing his own and pushing it away.

"Sorry," Calvin said. He stood up. His body seemed to be threatening to catch fire from the inside, currents and sparks were erupting from his stomach and chest, fluttering through his nerves in sudden jumps, dying and then starting again, making him feel again the spastic puppet, wired from the inside.

"Nervous."

"Don't know what's wrong with me," Calvin said, glancing around as he said it, half-expecting shadow friends of Johnny's to be gliding out, for whatever ritual needed to be performed.

"You got my hat on," Johnny said. "You can't hit a man when you're wearing his hat." He stood up, his arms outstretched.

"Don't."

"A man has to get his hat."

"Don't," Calvin said. The knife was in his hand, he was backing away. He sensed something behind him, stopped and looked. It was only a tree. Johnny Tulip walked slowly towards him, his arms still out, asking for his hat again. Calvin took the hat off his head, felt a quick cold band as the wind brushed through his hair, shooting through his scalp and the thousands of hollow tunnels of hairs. He hadn't even noticed the wind before. He pushed his hair back out of his eyes and then, carefully, tossed the hat to Johnny.

"Now the knife," Johnny said. "You couldn't take away a man's knife on his birthday."

Without the hat Calvin felt smaller, more vulnerable.

"Something's wrong with me," he said. He moved forward, could feel the cold where the dampness had seeped through his shoes, soaking his socks and feet.

"That's better."

"No."

"Sure," Johnny said. He was suddenly on top of him, wrapped about him, pinning Calvin's arms to his sides.

"No," Calvin said. His stomach had gone rigid and he could hear his voice coming from some place high up in his head. As he spoke his stomach tightened even more, the muscles knotted and cramped, blocking out everything else, then the pain crystallized, turned to wood, and he exploded, pushing out against Johnny, snapping his arms out like a rigid mannikin, smashing them into Johnny's chest and sending him falling into the clearing.

And Johnny, as he fell, felt his bones gathering closer together, his skeleton stiff with one birthday after another falling into the wet grass, the grass so long and so wet that it seemed to soak right through him as he let himself collapse onto his back. And look up to the sky where Orion, almost overhead, hung suspended on long invisible chains, suspended in the sky like a huge and grotesque mirror. Orion: the hunter's constellation was what the missionary had told him. But Johnny was never able to imagine the white men that the missionary showed him, strange white men in drawings in his books, white men covered in furs and crawling through the forest like make-believe machines, crawling through the forest carrying stones and stone clubs. The ancestors of us all, the missionary had said; but no Indian ever looked like that. And if the missionary didn't shoot a gun, it was only because he was afraid he would be knocked over by the recoil. Like his wife with her soft white belly and the line of black hair that stretched like a finger pointing from the middle of her belly to the slit

41

where she pushed him in so eagerly, gobbling him up as if she had already starved to death.

Then he coughed and the pain was so sharp that for a moment he thought it would end right then, on this one last disastrous birthday, his chest torn open and stripped away into raw bloody patches. And coughed again, sat up and hammered his hand into his chest, jolting whatever it was loose for one more moment. He looked up and saw that Calvin was leaning over him, his face white and frowning, a sick worried moon, his arm extended down.

Johnny grasped Calvin's hand, let the long arm swing him up onto his feet.

"I'm sorry," Calvin said.

Johnny laughed. Moved away from him and stood looking unsteadily down at the sea, rolling a cigarette. Now his bones felt stiffer than ever. Soon he would be like Victoria, frozen by the sea and by time. Soon they would find him somewhere, dead, turned into an old piece of wood. They wouldn't know whether to bury him or throw him away.

Four

Calvin's hand on Laurel Hobson's back made her spine feel like a long tunnel, a long hollow drum that sank in deeper with his every touch. Her father had always said that a person's body was like a map. So she had charted herself in his mind, two views, front and back, each two-page spreads in the atlas. When she was younger she had pictured her spine as the great west coast divide: a long range of mountains coloured red on the map, uniformly high and impenetrable.

There were bumps and scars but her body only came alive for her at random times and places, seeming to have nothing to do with any rhythm or will that she could master. The scars seemed to have no pattern either, were weeks and months of alcohol, morphine and cocaine mixed indistinguishably with the long wet winters, times when bodies and music could be brought into focus only briefly, then drifted away again under the force of the indifference that carried her from one summer to the next.

When she was young her spine was straight and supple. She could listen to her father talk and his words would be coming out of some story, the past and future unbroken. When they died it was easy. She had been expecting it without being able to say so. The funeral was easy too, coffins closed because of the accident, a warm Vancouver summer day and standing, watching William and Mary Hobson being buried together, William-and-Mary their friends had called them, making it one word, so it was proper, too, that they would die and be buried together, William-and-Mary Hobson. The earth was thrown over them and Laurel stood there, straight and sober, watching them disappear on this harmless day and feeling her past, suddenly, the moment she turned away, sealed off from her, thinking as she walked out of the cemetery and towards the road that somehow it fit that these endings had come together so inevitably: her first year of college and her first year away from home. And still, as she walked she felt nothing. Only vaguely empty and vaguely sad, planning to go up the coast for the summer and then back to university in the fall. She had stopped at the black iron gates of the cemetery to smell the flowers, May flowers, then guiltily started forward again, afraid that this was wrong.

Calvin's hand had found the place now, in the centre of her spine, the broken vertebra that was still swollen and spread out. His finger pressed against it but it wasn't sore anymore, overgrown and dull in fact, though when she was lying in bed and later up and bandaged waiting for it to heal there had been constant pain; she hadn't been able to turn or bend or move her upper arms or shoulders without being passed through this new centre that objected to everything.

His hand pushed back and forth, probing. She resisted the urge to move away, shifted back into him instead. But she hadn't displaced his hand. It still moved, slow and circling, as if sure that this careful reconnaissance would finally reveal something, press the secret button that would open the invisible door.

This sometimes seemed to be the way they shared this

bed. During the day he hung back but at night, whether or not they had sex or talked, when she was lying to sleep the way she always did, on her left side because then her heart would be facing up and down and she needed to go to sleep to the beating of her heart against the mattress, the last thing at night when her energy was completely spent, it seemed to her that Calvin's was renewed. He would curl around her and inspect her body with his hands, waiting for her to sleep, hunting her down in some way she didn't understand.

The first summer after the funeral, six years ago, she had helped her aunt pack the things in her parents' house and then had gone on the vacation, fulfilled the plan because, as even her aunt had said, there was no point staying and wishing things were different.

So she had gone north to the island with her girlfriend Louise. Both of them loaded down with tents and sleeping bags and heavy raincoats guaranteed for everything. Three days after they had set up their tent Johnny Tulip had found them there, sitting in their tent in the rain, unable to start a fire. Taken them home with him, found objects, to his mother and the houseful of related children and adults.

They had spent a week there; the memory of that time was now blocked by the constant drinking and everything that had happened afterwards. But the first and last nights were burned into her mind. The last night, when she had fooled herself with Johnny Tulip. And the first night, sitting at supper with Johnny Tulip's blind mother. And Victoria, Johnny's sister. Victoria who was almost ten years older than her and who jumped as soon as she came into the house, stared at her across the table, made her feel white and useless, stared at her resentfully until Laurel finally noticed, through her cold from the rain and the walking, that when they were both sitting at the strange shining table that was pushed into one corner of the living-room, their hands and wrists resting on the polished cedar, that when they both stretched out their hands and wrists their bones were like carbon copies of each other's, four hands, all the same, suddenly like mutated butterflies.

Victoria left that first night, the only time Laurel ever saw her alive. Her leaving somehow branded Laurel, made her of interest to all the Indians. And every day for a week Johnny Tulip escorted Laurel and Louise about the village, showing them off, white witches, parading them from kitchen to kitchen.

In each house she would see the work that the Indian women did. And in return, told them about her parents, named William-and-Mary, like the first King and Queen of England (which never seemed as funny as it was supposed to), her father a man who made maps so her mother did too: huge and intricate needlepoint maps that took years to sew, impressions of the old-style explorer maps that finally found walls in the houses of William Hobson's friends.

At night Johnny sometimes took them drinking and sometimes left them alone. Laurel slept on a broken blue couch on the verandah. The last night, Johnny Tulip came home late, drunk, morning already showing in the sky, low white mountains of light. Now Johnny Tulip was already past that invisible point that separates the young from the old. His forehead was high, and his hair greying. His long broken fingers played as well as they used to but no better. The lines in his face were carved so deep that when they were pushed out they had at their base long white shadows seldom touched by the sun. But six years ago he had been different, still living at his mother's house, forty-one years old and looking for a wife, his body intact and untouched by the doctors in Vancouver, still, despite everything, able to stay up for nights with only catnaps in the afternoon, drinking from before the sun began to set until the very end of the night, stopping only near dawn to stagger home and explore the house for food and money.

That last night he had not even been drinking seriously, at least he had said later, had only been out visiting and playing cards, making jokes about the virtue of the young white women who couldn't keep a fire in the rain and were staying at his mother's house. He was not desperately drunk, but he bounced off the back of the couch before settling carelessly on some combination of Laurel and her sleeping bag. Then sat with his hands folded staring out at the dirt road that ran through the village, down the hill to the cove where the Indians kept the remains of their boats. And where three totem poles from the old days still stood, all the colour washed off them, glaring east across the cove and towards the mainland in permanent disapproval of all that had come from that direction. Then he undid his hands and took out a cigarette, a short cork-filtered cigarette that was miraculously whole despite the crushed green package.

"Smoke?" Johnny Tulip had asked.

"No."

"You gotta relax," Johnny Tulip had said. And patted her on the shoulder, his hand firm and warm through the sleeping bag, the green sleeping bag William-and-Mary Hobson had given her one summer when all three of them had gone on a canoe trip, floating down the Thompson River to the place where it joined the Fraser, where the canyons got deeper and the water too fast.

"I'm okay."

"Me too," Johnny said.

"I am."

"Sure," Johnny said. "I was walking along the water tonight and a big bird flew down from the sky, a big square-winged hawk with a name it never says; and it landed on a round rock in front of me and spoke. 'Johnny Tulip,' it said, 'that white girl is making eyes at you.' "

"Go on."

"That's what I said," Johnny Tulip said. " 'Go on you big dumb bird.' I even threw a rock. 'That white girl is sad, is what's wrong with her.' "

"I'm okay."

"Me too," Johnny Tulip said. "Then that big dumb bird with the square wings kept right on following me as I walked down the beach. 'Johnny Tulip,' it said, 'you listen to me or I shit on your head.' So, what could I do? Only a fool lets a bird shit on him at night."

"Birds only go to the bathroom during the day."

"You should have been with me," Johnny Tulip said. "Indians don't know nothing." He was leaning against the couch, talking. She could feel his back and arms through the sleeping bag. She wondered what he would look like, standing naked against the morning sky. Whether he would undress first or make her come in the house with him. "Then that damned bird started at me again," Johnny Tulip said. "He's a big old bird and his breath is awful." He was bent forward. She followed him, her knees against his back. He unzipped the sleeping bag and slid his hand between her legs. It was unexpected. His hand was calloused and rough, felt like sandpaper against her skin. "Big old hawk was right," Johnny said.

"Hurry up." She pulled him into the sleeping bag, on top of her. His pants were open and half-pulled down. She could feel the buckle of his belt biting into her knees. Nothing else. Johnny Tulip smelled like beer and tobacco and cedar smoke.

"You're closed up tight," Johnny Tulip said. "Like a clam."

"I'm sorry." But she felt relieved too and started

wondering how they would divide up into two people again, extricate themselves from the embarrassing remains of this night. Then he pushed and she could feel him inside her.

"Big bird said to take you by surprise."

"You're not supposed to talk," Laurel said. She wrapped her legs around him, the way she had read about. He pushed deeper, pulsed briefly, then was finished. He climbed out of the sleeping bag. Laurel got out too, and squatted on the front lawn. The mountains of light had grown, stretched half-way up the sky, turned the rest blue. All the stars were gone but the moon was still visible. While she waited she looked down at the ground. She could see only a small streak of blood, running like a vein from her calf to her ankle. Johnny Tulip was standing on the porch, pissing through a gap in the railing.

"Did it hurt?"

"No." It was too fast, she wanted to say, but didn't. She wondered if it would be all right now, to put on her clothes. In a way she wanted to do it again, to see if it would take longer, if she would feel enough to have something to remember. Her body reacted to the cold suddenly; goose pimples snapped out all over her. She stood up, jumped back onto the porch and pulled on her socks, her underpants and jeans. Stood briefly with her arms crossed over her chest and then put on a skirt and sweater.

"It gets better," Johnny Tulip said.

"I liked it. Really. May a bird shit on my head if I'm lying."

"Yeah," Johnny said. "It was okay."

Putting on her clothes and sitting on the couch while Johnny went in to make coffee she had speculated about the way William-and-Mary had done it the first time. She could never really believe they did it at all. Certainly not when she was older and William slept in his study with his maps and his books, the bed buried beneath papers and ashtrays so thick that Mary Hobson used to come in every night and rescue it for him, turning on a lamp with three see-through princes painted onto the base and a shade that was yellowed. Like human skin Laurel would say, from some expedition; but her father insisted that it was only a special kind of paper.

He had blue eyes, William Hobson, so had his wife. But Laurel's were dark brown, right from the day she was born. Her parents' eyes aged from deep blue, like this dawn sky, to green-blue and brown-blue as they got older, making her wonder if their eyes were turning brown with all the bits of rot that were circulating through their bodies.

After the funeral her aunt gave her the old album she had of their pictures and while she was waiting for Johnny Tulip's coffee she thought of the album, trying to remember what had come first, her mother riding no-hands down some unidentified Vancouver hill, the street lined with trees, not houses, a detail that seemed somehow allied with the innocent youth of her mother, or her father standing on his head, his baggy trousers slid down to his knees, revealing socks held up by garters and a scar on one leg that stretched its whole visible length.

Johnny made the coffee the way everyone on this island did, boiling the grounds in the pot and then pouring it out slowly and hopefully. When he served it to her, sweetened with sugar and condensed milk, so hot it seemed almost boiling still, she could see tiny black specks on the surface of the coffee, feel them grate against her tongue as it burned its way down her throat, into her stomach which felt suddenly empty. She stood up to adjust her clothes and there was a quick warm liquid spilling from her insides down her thigh, making her want to know how he could have put so much inside her, so quickly, or maybe this was good, meant she wouldn't get pregnant. She was shaking herself, pressing her thighs together and hoping that her jeans could absorb this weird stuff when her girlfriend Louise came out of the house, also holding a cup of coffee.

Calvin's hand had stopped now, finally given up, was resting flat and warm on her back. She could hear his breathing slow down, deepen. As he fell asleep she would start to wake up, helplessly, floating on the edge of her bed in this new low state that their being together had invented, without enough energy to get up and read, or even to push him back to his own side of the bed when he began to dream and fling himself about. Sometimes she had tried to talk to him when they were like this, but it was no use. Even when he was, she was sure, wide awake and exploring her body, he would pretend to be asleep, answer her questions in grunts and turn away from her.

The heel of his hand was stopped on the place where her spine had been cracked, only twenty-four hours after she had let Johnny Tulip into her sleeping bag; knowing even as she lost her balance and had started to slide down the cliff that these two incidents were somehow related, that now whatever had been started on Johnny Tulip's porch was being finished. At first it hadn't even hurt; she had just lain still, come to a halt on a small plateau of sand and rocks. It was only when she tried to move that she felt anything at all, a small pain that was too insignificant to explain the numbness that had spread from her neck to her waist, pinned her down, reminded her suddenly of all the fantasies she had had when she had first thought about sex, long intricate plays alternating between quick dramas where she was the dominant amazon queen, six feet tall and stronger than all the men she ordered to perform various acts on her, always ineffectually as it turned out; and lingering scenes in which she was thin and limp and passive, slave to the huge muscled ape-men who wore black nylon stockings over their heads and were always on the verge of penetrating her in ways so awful that she was incapable of imagining the details, preferring instead to concentrate on the horrible and insatiable moaning that would be coming from her lipsticked lips, sounding and looking amazingly like those that issued forth from the women in magazines she had seen, but more real and extravagant, so heart-rending that finally the men would be driven from the room by them and she would be left alone, surrounded by the instruments of passion.

But this time when she had opened her eyes there was only the sky and the sea, and there was no one to hear her. So she had tried to roll over, to get on her feet again, but couldn't move at all, could do nothing but call out for help.

They took her to the plane and let her ride on a stretcher, a long ride all the way down to Vancouver. The stewardess gave her a needle and she flew up with the clouds, forgave the nightmare trip from the beach to the airport, forgave everything except the enormous white puffy clouds they were flying through, huge white clouds and she could see how perfect it would be to live in the sky, to bounce about from cloud to cloud, sleeping curled up in a white serrated space. And when they got to the hospital she asked for another shot. She didn't remember being shaven and wrapped in bandages, just lay wherever they put her and sailed back up in the clouds, higher still, up to the place where they made the clouds in a silver castle with silver cannon that shot them out into the sky. Where they made strange music when they bounced off each other, a music of colours and sounds that took place inside her head, played through the bones of her skull and all the tiny networks in her brain that she could feel lighting up in perpetually changing sequences like a great carnival of rides and lights. BOING BOING she sang, keeping her brain company, the nurse telling her afterwards that she had spent the whole night singing BOING BOING and snapping her fingers until the resident told her to cut down on the morphine, after all, they didn't even know if she could afford to pay.

The next morning they had shown her the X-rays. Her spine came in a long chain, like the spine of a fish. But one of the pieces showed a crack, though she wouldn't have noticed it if they hadn't pointed it out to her, couldn't feel exactly where it was through the bandages that held her whole back rigid and, with the help of another needle she found she could move everything again, everything that stuck out anyway, arms and legs and neck, enough to notice they had stuffed a kotex between her legs.

Louise had come back with her on the plane too. But Laurel had no memory of her there or at night in the hospital, only the morning when they had shown her the X-rays and then let her in, transformed out of her island jeans and sweatshirt to her normal Vancouver costume.

"I didn't tell your aunt," was the first thing Louise said. She had huge innocent eyes that had never changed since she was a child, eyes that even William-and-Mary had trusted totally, never suspecting that she was initiating Laurel into all the minor sins they could think of: smoking and drinking and going downtown after school to see what would happen if they stood outside bars, watching how the prostitutes on Granville Street did it, sliding unobtrusively out of doorways and hooking their arm into the elbow of some passerby, as if he was someone they knew, then, shortly afterwards, turning back with this same man and going back to the hotel, this long-lost acquaintance having forgotten something, reappearing a few minutes or even an hour later, wearing the same clothes, all made up again and ready to start over.

"Does it hurt?"

"No."

"I thought it would hurt," Louise said. "Johnny came with us all the way to the airport."

"Gee."

"I guess you're kind of dumb when you're all doped up."

"I am a thin white streak through history. Look at my works, oh ye mighty, and despair."

"Maybe I better tell your aunt."

"No," Laurel protested, struggling to sit up but her back was completely stiffened by the bandages and she could only push part way up with her arms and fall down.

"Are you okay?"

"Sure," Laurel said. "I feel like a rabbit that's been run over by a truck."

"You look kind of awful."

"Don't tell my aunt."

"Okay." The nurse came into the room with her big ruled notebook and a tray of pills. Laurel took the pills, winced as she put her head back to swallow them.

"You can have another needle if you want," the nurse said.

"Please."

"Some people don't like it."

"I don't mind."

"It should start feeling better in a day or two." She had the rubber wrapped around Laurel's arm, twisted tight. "You've got great veins for a junkie," the nurse said. "Nice and easy." The needle was still in her arm when she felt it hit, flowing through her body, making everything sweet and solid. She kept her eyes open, watched Louise look away as the needle went in. When she looked back her eyes seemed bigger than ever, threatening to sprout right out of her head on long antennae.

54

"They said you'd be all right in a few weeks," Louise said, after the nurse had left.

"Sure."

"You're really lucky."

"I am a thin white streak through history and God is on my side."

"You could get addicted to that stuff, you know."

"Don't be stupid."

"My mother had a friend who got addicted. It was horrible."

"Oh no."

"It *was.*"

"Of course," Laurel said. She didn't know whether to tell Louise that she was safe now, that her eyes were back in her head where they belonged. She could see Louise fiddling with her purse, wondering if it would be all right to smoke. Louise's hands were white and round, like her face, like all of Louise that was made up of different size balls pasted together. William Hobson had been partial to Louise's rounds, had always hung about when she was visiting, told his awful jokes to her and insisted on giving her maps every Christmas. Laurel had only seen Louise's father once or twice. He was thin and like dry vinegar compared to Louise. He never came upstairs except to get the beer out of the refrigerator and then take it back down to the basement, where he had been perfecting the same bookcase for three years. Once when he wasn't home, Laurel had made Louise take her down there. They had seen, under the workbench and lined up in neat rows beside the furnace, opened and empty tins of spaghetti and beans.

"I guess we'll get him put away sometime," Louise said.

"He's not that bad."

"He's sort of creepy at night," Louise said, but didn't elaborate. Louise's mother was even rounder than Louise, not fat but just devoid of all straight lines. Her bedroom somehow reflected this, the plump quilted bedspread, deep red, redder than anything in the Hobson household, and a naked clay angel that stood in the corner, with a plant growing out a hole in the top of its head.

Louise came to visit her in the hospital every day, through the whole summer, leaving only once to go up to the islands to collect their things. Finally, as the days turned into weeks and months, Laurel's aunt had to be told.

When her aunt came to the hospital Laurel had been prepared to be lectured for her selfishness and irresponsibility. She wasn't ready for the way her aunt marched into the room, took a look at her, and pronounced her not only numb in the back but thin and suffering from malnutrition, pimples and moral decay, producing a sudden burst of Jehovah's Witness pamphlets and insisting not only that Laurel leave the hospital, but quit taking all drugs. "You don't have to do what she says," Louise told her, "you can come and stay with us." But she didn't. She went instead to her aunt's and watched the remainder of the summer from the bathtub, where she sat every day, hoping that the hot water would fill the gap the morphine had left, smoking the cigarettes and drinking the Southern Comfort that Louise smuggled to her, the Southern Comfort blending with the steam and making everything bearable, but not really touching the anxiety that seemed to have permeated her whole body.

By this time her bandage had been reduced and could be protected by three plastic dry-cleaning bags tied at her stomach and neck, bags that ballooned up as she sat in the water so she would cover them with suds and chatter to herself in her aunt's voice, swearing to go on a jello diet, wondering why it was they puffed up in the bath but then, when she got out, hung slack and wet like old flesh, so she would tear them off her and, hiding the bottle and the cigarettes in her towel, walk carefully to her room and prepare for yet another evening that was hung-over and restless, reading the endless supply of mystery novels that her aunt had stored in the attic after her conversion, watching the television in her room, sometimes even venturing as far as the backyard where her aunt would set up two deckchairs and read to her from the Bible, selected parables whose meaning all escaped her, and tell Laurel how unfortunate it was that her mother had married an agnostic, who was no better than an atheist in God's eyes, and that surely things would have been different if they had believed. After all, she said once, as if it shouldn't have been necessary and would never be mentioned again, William-and-Mary Hobson had been killed on a Sunday, when they were driving for pleasure, an excursion that would not have even happened if they had been on their way to or from church.

In the fall Laurel had registered for her second year at the university. She sat in front of the new library, filling out forms and watching the other students marching diligently back and forth in their new plaid logging jackets. All of them were clear of purpose in a way that escaped her, couldn't touch her at all despite the monument behind her, a tower high enough to be seen from everywhere on the campus, crowned by a clock so that none need be ignorant of the exact point to which the day had progressed.

While he slept Calvin's body would twist and jerk spasmodically, beginning as he was drifting off, continuing in fits and starts throughout the night. Sometimes his flailing elbows caught her in the face or stomach so that in annoyance she would hit him back. But he never seemed to mind, just turned away and resumed dreaming. In the morning he woke with lines around his eyes as if he had been putting himself through endless inquisitions and confessions. The way he moved when he first got up was like an old man, hobbled and half-paralyzed he had to curl up in himself and drink coffee before he could even touch food. Sometimes she thought she could almost see the gap in him, a canyon running up the middle of his body that had been opened when he left the east, feeling, she was sure, the same way she had felt going back to school that year, when she couldn't even complete the formalities of registration but walked down to the beach instead, day after day, to sit on fat driftwood logs and mindlessly watch the water.

She had felt broken then; there seemed to be something she needed that she couldn't eat or drink or smoke or even get from other people, a need trapped in her like a sliver or a hangnail. Finally she had had to give up on the university and one day flew back to the island, carrying her pack and her father's old rifle. And hiked back up to the cliff where she had fallen. This time she slid down easily, there was nothing difficult at all. And when she had followed the trail at the bottom for a mile she came to an abandoned cabin with a lock that was easy to break.

Five

Laurel slid carefully out of the bed, pushing the sleeping bag and her pillow into Calvin's back as she moved. Then she took the extra blanket and wrapped it around herself. The fire was almost completely out, only grey-red ashes remained. She added a few sticks of kindling and a new log. While waiting for the wood to catch, she smoked a cigarette, feeling for once that her consciousness was clear and focused, the line between cold and warm slowly moving through her.

The cigarette smoke seemed to stick in her lungs these days. The tar and the nicotine had now established permanent deposits and the smoke circulated more sluggishly, formed into clouds, clinging to her insides and refusing to be easily exhaled. When she was in the hospital there had been a man down the hall who was having his lung removed. They had cut him open, a long sweeping cut that went from his neck down to his belly, round his waist and ribs, and up his back again. It would be better to die all at once, like William-and-Mary, without going to the hospital and having the dead parts cut away, a little more each time, until what was left could no longer survive. But Johnny Tulip had let them open him up staying down in

Vancouver for six weeks one winter. There had been snow that winter too; and when he came back she would go to visit him at his blind mother's house. They would sit on the front verandah and look at the snow across the bay on the mountains, what was left of it melting quickly with the sun and the rains. Every day they watched it shrink and flatten out, like a big upside-down bowl of ice cream, Johnny Tulip had said, deciding he was almost better and that, when it was gone, his cure would be complete.

In the mornings when she got up and started the fire, Laurel would promise herself that they would get something proper to heat this cabin, something other than this old kitchen stove which took only tiny pieces of wood. Though it had been burning all evening and there was a new fire in it, the outer reaches of the stove were only mildly warm. But the rail that ran along its front was fat and perfect for her feet. She propped herself up in her chair, pushed deeper into her blanket, listened to the fire pick up speed through the half-opened grates, the fresh-cut cedar hissing as it dried.

Now that she was finally out of bed, she was glad to be awake. Calvin seemed to need more sleep; even when he was up he stumbled around half the time as if he was dreaming. He seemed able to go through whole series of days without ever really being awake, noticing what was happening around him, as if his energy was all off somewhere else, swirling about in lazy circles. She thought about lighting the kerosene lamp. Calvin had given her a science fiction book about a world where people were only allowed to speak one day a week. In the hospital, she had wondered what it would be like to pretend she couldn't talk.

William Hobson could never have lived without words. Even his maps were more real to him than the places they represented. In a canoe he could sit with a big drawing board across his knees, sketching the shape of the river as they floated. They always picked routes which had the current do the work, and at night, by the campfire, he would re-live the day's adventure, poring over the pictures he had drawn. When he had assembled a map of everywhere they had passed, he would check it over with a real map, one from a book, and correct his so that it was the same. Mary Hobson's maps were different. They were huge dense representations of nowhere, seas shifting carelessly into continents, rivers of thread running down the centre of land masses and then inexplicably changing direction and careening off into some sudden red or purple lake. In the book people were allowed to use sign language on the days they didn't talk. So words were still everywhere, sealing off the world and substituting names for things, sounds for feelings, turning everything into instant history that could be recorded and filed.

The fire and the blanket had made her warm but not drowsy. The sky was clear again, Johnny Tulip's birthday having brought this change of weather that had lasted three days now, and through the window she could see a few stars. She got up and walked over to the cupboards above the sink, hesitated, then took out the bottle of rye Johnny Tulip had brought to her on his birthday. She could hear the bed creaking from the next room, turned and looked through the doorway. Calvin was spread-eagled diagonally across the bed, an arm drooping off one corner and a foot hanging down from the end. Laurel put on her jeans, stretched high into the air. In this cabin the ceiling was so low she could touch it if she stretched, push her back into place. When she went home from the hospital they had given her exercises to strengthen her back, but the only one she was interested in was standing on her hands. She had practised it all winter on the island and the next summer, when Louise came up to visit her with her lawyer boyfriend, she had been able to walk on her hands, from the beach and into the ocean until the water had splashed into her face and knocked her over.

In the light of the fire the rye was warm and amber. The look of a full bottle always fascinated her, the way it insisted on being started. But she could never quite get used to the taste of the first drink, delayed it by pushing her tongue against the mouth of the bottle until the burning was unbearable and she had to pull it away and swallow the rye, still burning, tracing its path through her throat and into her stomach where it burned again, hurt too, always on the first drink, a flash of pain sent up her stomach and into her ribs, the alcohol triggering off something else that could only be eased by another drink. She put on her shirt and then Calvin's sweater. She liked his clothes, especially this sweater, green and blue with patches where the elbows had worn away. The patches carefully and expertly blended in. It was easy to see the whole areas this perfect mender had excised from his existence, all the things he couldn't and wouldn't do, not even thinking about it but in a total unawareness as if the supply and maintenance of the household was something that happened of its own accord, one of the laws of nature, which should never, as William Hobson was fond of repeating endlessly, be contravened.

William Hobson had always matched himself perfectly to his circumstances, especially his wife. He was, in his black leather shoes, the same height as his wife in her heels. A small man whose smallness had only really registered when Laurel saw that his coffin was no longer than Mary Hobson's; William-and-Mary buried in identical coffins, even the same stainless steel trim around the edges, like twins. The coffins had been closed but years later she had seen their faces in her dreams, crudely repaired and made up. William Hobson's skin was powdered to hide the black bristles that he could never shave quite smooth, that were scratchy in one direction in the morning and both directions by night-time. Mary Hobson was powdered smooth too; but the most important thing had been her hair, parted down the middle, grey brown, curving out from her neck, and lacquered into tiny angel's wings to carry her to heaven.

Laurel Hobson stepped into her moccasins and went outside. Standing beside the cabin she could smell the smoke from the fire, drifting slowly, feel the cold air circling her wrists and ankles. The moon shone through these young trees, sent long black shadows criss-crossing on the ground. She could see where it was brighter too, past the trees, and walked out towards the dunes. The sand was cold but soft. She pushed and dug until she had made herself a seat and could look out towards the ocean. She took her second drink then, her body close upon itself in the dark. This time the rye swam down smoothly, settling home in her belly, dissolving the dead faces of William-and-Mary, leaving her alive with the ocean breathing slowly into the sand, sounds of water, and with them, high and barely distinct, the sound of gravel crunching under shoes, Johnny Tulip's uneven step as he walked along the high-water mark.

She stood up to meet him, uncapping the bottle and taking her third drink, holding its bottom end high and pointing it at the nose of the moon. Calvin didn't like her to drink. He would never say so directly, but only asked her over and over what it was that it did for her, though he himself thought nothing of getting drunk on beer and being sick half the night afterwards, going off somewhere with Johnny Tulip and staying there even after Johnny had left, staying until she had come and found him and dragged him back to the truck, having to stop every few minutes while he was sick, finally driving him back to the cabin and watching him tear off his clothes and go splashing into the sea to sober up. So cold afterwards that he could hardly come inside her, shivering like a drowned animal the whole time. And when it was over he only wanted to keep lying on top of her, to get warm.

"It's war," Johnny Tulip said, as he pulled up in front of her, stopped, took the bottle from behind her back. Now that he was forty-seven Johnny Tulip was the same age William Hobson had been when he died. He was short too, like William Hobson. But William Hobson's face had hardly been lined at all, a few small creases near his mouth and eyes, and more across his forehead. He had stayed thin and always seemed to smell of soap and powders. But somehow the effect had not been to make him seem younger but older, a perfectly preserved seventy-year-old, not like Johnny Tulip who was a total disaster, his face pushed in and scarred, lines and wrinkles running everywhere, his front teeth showing whole and white but his molars all missing on one side so that one cheek could be seen to be slowly collapsing into the shadows. The bones beneath his eyes were wide and prominent. They were knicked with small scars, small white lines of thickened flesh, tiny scars like the ones that showed in two places above his eyebrows too, as if they had happened at the same time.

A slow small wind had come up, sweeping across the beach, not foreboding but present, announcing that with it would come a change in weather, a return to the usual rain. But still the sky was clear; there was only a thin rim of haze along the horizon.

Johnny handed the bottle back to Laurel and sat down on the beach. He had his legs crossed and his chin propped up in his hands. He looked so unlike himself that Laurel couldn't help laughing.

"What's so funny?" Johnny asked. He squirmed about and changed position, lying on his side and looking awkwardly out at the ocean. Then he stood up and walked about uncomfortably, his hands behind his back, starting and stopping every few seconds, always about to speak but never saying anything.

"He can't help it," Laurel said, still laughing.

"Ohhh," Johnny moaned, "I can't help it, mama." He rearranged himself and pounded his chest with his fists, making himself cough as he hit himself. "Goddamn," Johnny Tulip said.

Laurel's throat tightened: Johnny Tulip, forty-seven years old, was out of control coughing now, bent over and almost retching, his face red even in the moonlight, the unlit cigarette still in his mouth, shaking crazily with each spasm. When she was with him, she kept feeling that he was going to die this winter. Ever since coming back from Vancouver with Calvin he had seemed this way, too sick to live through another six months of rain and snow wearing his usual leaky old shoes, drinking himself half to death every night, even now, his hand reaching out for the bottle which she instinctively held away from him, then, as always, gave in. But this time he just took a small swallow, holding it in his throat, she knew, for the cough, the same thing that was killing him now his only medicine.

"The bar," Johnny said, clearing his throat and straightening himself.

"It must be closed," Laurel said.

"No." Johnny coughed again, this time lightly, spat and cleared his throat. He walked a few steps down the beach, as if to get away from the last minutes, brushed off his coat and rubbed his long broken hands together. "You remember the government men in the bar?"

"Sure," Laurel said. After Johnny and Calvin had left one of the men had come and sat beside her, dressed in his dry-cleaned grey suit with a white dry-cleaners handkerchief in the pocket. "One for show and one for blow,"

William Hobson had called the handkerchief trick, preferring himself to take pills for his allergies and wear sports
jackets with a plastic case of pens in the pocket.

The government man had bought a drink for her and,
instead of trying to pick her up or ask where he could find a
moose or deer to kill, questioned her about the logging
company.

"They gave the company a new timber lease," Johnny
said. "Pretty soon they'll take down the whole island."

He scraped his shoes against the wet stones. Soon the
company would invent new machines that could process the
whole island at once, complex metal mouths that could
digest the wood and minerals instantly, spit them out onto
ships and then stand and wait, rusting and still, a new kind
of totem pole waiting for the next crop of trees.

He had started walking along the beach, back towards
the road. Laurel followed him automatically, walking, as
she always did, between him and the water, for no reason at
all except that Johnny had once mentioned he didn't like
water. And, in fact, she had never seen him swim, had never
seen any Indian or white person born on this island swim.
She noticed now that he had a canvas bag over one
shoulder; it was small but seemed heavy, banged rather
than flapped against his side. And he had something in his
jacket pocket too. At first she had assumed it was a bottle
but now saw it was metal, a flashlight.

On the beach Johnny walked as he always did, unevenly and with so much difficulty that she wanted to tell him to
stop, to come back to the cabin and sleep. But when they
turned into the forest he was as he used to be, walking
quickly and surely through the underbrush. She had to run
to keep up with him, couldn't help stumbling sometimes on
roots and stones that she couldn't see, the trees dense and
mature here, letting no moonlight through so she couldn't

see anything at all except Johnny's silhouette, moving swiftly ahead of her.

There was a highway that bisected the island, running from the airport at the southern tip up to the town on the north shore with the hotel and the houses where the logging management lived. The eastern side of the island curved inwards. And within that curve were small coves and inlets where some of the old Indian villages had been located. The road met the coast where it swept in: so they could drive the truck from the cabin to the town, by going along the beach at low tide to an old logging road that climbed through some forest to the highway. But on foot there were countless minor variations of the route and Johnny Tulip seemed to take a different one every time they were together, plunging in at random and instinctively finding old deer trails that finally came out at the road.

In winter it was difficult, almost impossible to drive the truck up the beach because the winds carried the tides higher, washed out the usual paths the truck followed and swelled the streams that ran across the beach into the ocean making them too deep to cross. So, once it was fixed, Calvin had left the truck parked at the road. Tonight Laurel had thought Johnny would be leading her there, that he had somehow got himself stranded and wanted to be driven back to his house. But he went at a strange slant through the forest, taking a much longer way than usual and when they came out, finally, they were miles north of the truck.

"It would be bad luck to drive," Johnny Tulip said. They were on the road, at the top of a hill, and could see for a few hundred yards in each direction. The moon had climbed higher, and after the darkness of the forest seemed completely bright, almost as bright as day, making long black shadows that pointed north. They started walking along the road, following their shadows, sometimes so

67

exactly they seemed to be stepping into them. Laurel felt totally awake. The walking was making her warm. She pulled the sleeves of Calvin's sweater up to her elbows, held it out and waved it at the waist to let the air in. Calvin was much bigger and heavier than her. His sweater fit only loosely, the arms coming out over her hands and the bottom down to her thighs. With the sweater held out it seemed huge, made her look six months pregnant. She tried to imagine how it was going to be, the inside of that huge space filled and swollen with fluids, pulling out at her spine and pushing everything out of place. She had thought she was pregnant twice, neither by choice, and had miscarried early both times, sick for a week with what seemed to be an endless explosion of cramps and blood.

She was hungry now, and thirsty too. She let Johnny get ahead and could see by the way his jacket moved that he had only the flashlight with him. "You forgot the bottle," Laurel said.

Johnny patted his coat and shrugged. "Can't trust an old drunk," he said. But she knew he had done it on purpose, taking the bottle from her and drinking from it so he could fool her and leave it on the beach before they set out. She wondered if he saw her the same way she saw him, sick and broken from drink, too sick to even last the winter. There was no mirror at the cabin, she hated mirrors, but at the bar she had looked in the mirror when she went to the bathroom. Her face was exactly as always. No wrinkles or lines anywhere, the skin taut as it should be, as if she would stay this way forever. The bodies of women who had babies were permanently changed, with stretch marks on their stomachs and breasts. One of Johnny's sisters was married, with children. Even Mary Gail had had one child, though it didn't survive. She suddenly wanted to be back in bed with Calvin, trapped by both their needs for sleep, the warmth of his body and the way he somehow, she was sure he was unaware of it himself, was able to move right by her defences, effortlessly, as if his presence was sufficient to render them inoperative. She had stopped taking birth control pills after meeting him, without telling him. The first night he had asked if it was all right and she had told him yes, not specifying how or what, and since then he had never mentioned the subject. She wondered what he would think if he woke up and found she wasn't there. Maybe nothing, lately he had seemed so stunned and slow that she had started to wonder if he was actually quite stupid and only used his silence to cover it up.

They were walking fast and even though she knew the road well, had gone up and down it hundreds of times, it was hard for her to tell exactly where they were. It seemed to have been almost two hours since they had started out and in the time they were walking Johnny had hardly spoken.

He stopped abruptly, holding her arm and motioning her to be quiet. The night was exceptionally still. She realized that she was hearing almost nothing: no wind, no deer, not even the sounds of birds. Johnny Tulip turned towards her. His eyes were bright, almost luminescent. His eyes and his hand were fastened to her, dug in like claws.

"Listen," he said. His voice rasped. The wind came up again as he spoke. The road was a hollow slash through the forest and the air rushed down it, whistling through this channel in the trees. Along with the wind was something else, a low consistent sound that seemed to be almost humming.

"It's just a car," Laurel whispered. She didn't know why she was whispering. She started off the road, climbing a small hill that led into the forest. By the time they were hidden they could hear it clearly, its engine whining in the night. Then its headlights became visible on the horizon. The closer it got, the higher-pitched was the sound of its motor and tires. There were so few cars on the island that Laurel recognized most of them. But this one was new to her, and when it came up to them she realized she hadn't seen it before, a long black hearse with its inside lights on, C.W. Smith driving it at a hundred miles an hour, the government man who had talked to her in the bar sitting up front, the other government men and Mary Gail in the back. All of them drinking beer and listening to the radio, turned up full volume.

"Look at that," Johnny said. "It's a hearse. It came over on the ferry yesterday afternoon." It was complete with flags mounted on the front and rear fenders. The sound deepened just as it passed them, then began to fade. They stayed crouched in the edge of the forest, listening to it recede. The wind seemed to have passed with the car. It always started like this after a few clear days, slowly and in gusts. By tomorrow it would be blowing hard and steady along the beach. In the afternoon or evening it would rain.

"Come on," Johnny said. He stood up and started walking again, not towards the road but further into the trees. They had to keep climbing for a few minutes. Then it levelled off and there was a good trail. After about a mile Johnny stopped. They were no longer in forest but in second growth bush. The trees were thinner and there was less space between them. Johnny took the flashlight out for the first time, snapped it on briefly and put it back in his pocket. The light had shown an old logging road, running straight ahead, starting to sprout seedlings and bushes in the centre hump but the wheelruts permanently dead, still almost totally free from vegetation after twenty years.

"Look," Laurel said. She took the light and shone it again on the ruts of the old road. They were filled with tracks.

"Lots of deer up here," Johnny Tulip said. "This is the road where my father died." He had told her about it once, only on being asked, how his father had decided that the logging company had made it impossible to live on the island so he had signed up to work for them, clearing a road, and had one day said good-bye to his family, so much like the rest of his odd jokes that they had hardly paid attention, and then gone to the place he was working and felled a tree, right on top of himself. When they found him he was lying with his head beneath the trunk, kneeling forward and offering himself just like the Catholic King in the schoolbooks the missionaries had shown them.

"It was just up here," Johnny Tulip said, walking forward a few steps, shining the light until it stopped at a huge old stump, eight feet across. There was a noise from the underbrush. They froze.

Johnny slowly swept the light along the side of the road. A doe moved unconcernedly onto the old trail, stood sideways to them and poked her head along the surface of a salmonberry bush that was growing beside where Johnny's father had been killed. It was a large doe, still warm with sleep and Laurel could smell the heat coming off her.

Johnny had his arm out, barring her way. But then he moved forward, towards the doe, the light still on but pointed at the ground. The doe turned her head briefly, her eyes sliding gold-green into the light and then away again as she went back to the berries. Johnny kept moving forward, each step tiny and soundless, his one arm holding the light and the other stretched out, like a tightrope walker. Laurel became aware that he was making some sort of noise in the back of his throat, a low noise barely audible, so quiet and low that she didn't know if he was making it on purpose or having trouble breathing. But then it rose and fell like the echo of a song. Even though the doe had started out only ten yards away Johnny was moving so slowly that he still wasn't there. The doe scratched her back feet. A tremour passed along her spine. Laurel couldn't bear to keep standing in this same position, began to lower herself so she could crouch on the ground and wait. As her hands met the earth it was unexpectedly cold, the old road grown over by only the thinnest layer of uneven grass and moss, now losing the last of its summer heat to these clear skies.

The doe turned to Johnny again. Her eyes pulsed in the light, expanding and contracting to the beat of her heart, the green deepening as the blood was pushed through it, and Laurel could feel her own heart drumming in time with the doe, so scared that the fear and the beating of her heart weren't things that were part of her but had become everything, her body pounding in time with the pulsing of the doe's eyes, the light from her eyes now seeming much brighter, coming from somewhere inside the head and passing through the irises as through a shattered crystal window, passing through the doe's eyes and through Laurel's eyes to some place in the back of her brain which now started to pulse too, pushing its answering signals back into the night, towards the doe, which now, still looking straight at her, rubbed her neck along Johnny Tulip's sleeve, then, suddenly, startled, leaped it seemed straight up in the air, its front hooves flashing forward like small sharp jewels. Then the doe was coming right at her and Laurel was pushing herself up, her fingers pushing off the cold ground and just brushing against the doe's fur as it swept by, its feet somehow missing her as it passed her. In one bound it was off the road, crashed briefly into the underbrush and then was silent, swallowed by the darkness.

Something in her seemed to have turned wild. Her whole body was still pounding with her heart and she wondered if it was true, that she had been drinking so much she was sick and now would have a heart attack and die here, on this old road that was going nowhere anyway, poor Johnny, he would have to carry her out and explain everything to Calvin. Even without the light it seemed brighter now than it had before. The moon was directly overhead and she could see Johnny, still standing in the place his father had stood, leaning casually against the stump as if he were in a bar, waiting. There was still no noise. The doe must have stopped. But Laurel didn't want to follow it. She felt like she used to when Johnny first took her for walks on this island, impossibly clumsy and stupid, incapable of hearing or seeing or smelling anything, walking around, Johnny used to say, like she had a bag on her head.

She looked at Johnny again and he still hadn't moved. She felt she had been inexcusably clumsy, missed a chance for something she couldn't name or place. When she first came there had at least been the excuse that she was strange to the island. Now it was only her whiteness that had made the doe attack her, the armies and cities that were exuded from her blood, that nothing would erase. She felt suddenly like William Hobson, a truculent foreigner determined to have something to take home.

The light from the moon was beginning to waver, thin torn veils of cloud dimmed it sporadically, announced again that soon it would begin to rain, that the island would be blanketed by the usual mist and endless further layers of cloud until they were so thick that even the sun would be barely distinct most days, only a diffused brightness moving across the southern sky, waiting for summer to raise it up again.

Laurel felt cold now. She had her hands balled into fists, the long sleeves of Calvin's sweater pulled over them. She was still facing in the direction that the doe had fled. She could hardly remember being in bed with Calvin, the rye that had long been soaked into blood and burned away by the walking. She felt tired, not exhausted but defeated.

"She liked you," Johnny said.

"What?"

"The doe liked you. But she was afraid of you too."

"Sure," Laurel said. "Maybe I reminded her of her mother."

"She liked you."

"You said that." Laurel's feet had come unstuck. She walked towards Johnny. "Give me a cigarette."

"You shouldn't smoke in the woods. You might start a fire."

"Okay," Laurel said. She patted his jacket until she found the package. Taking out the cigarette and lighting it helped her get composed. She wondered what she would do if she didn't smoke. Chewing twenty sticks of gum a day wouldn't be the same. Johnny was smoking too. It was unusual, in fact, for him to be carrying ready-mades. He had a leather pouch one of his sisters had given him and most of the time he carried tobacco and papers. And, when it was available, in a plastic bag separate from the tobacco, the dope that his mother grew in the garden, bright green.

Johnny had started walking again, slowly, down the old logging road that seemed to get easier to see and clearer as they progressed. She hooked her hand into his arm as they walked.

"Are we going to the movies?"

"Double feature," Johnny said. "First show is Dracula And The Deer."

"And the second?"

"Great San Francisco Fire," Johnny said. "God gets his revenge and burns the sinners in their false church."

"Oh." The road they had been walking on connected to another wider old road, also disused for years, but it had been graded flat so instead of walking in the ruts they could go anywhere. It was all dead and packed with gravel; even the moss could hardly grow here. Once they saw another deer ahead of them. Just a shadow, its antlers coming out of its head like thin and elegant antennae, two for each side.

The first road had been one of many branch roads that

flowed into this main, wider one. Soon the whole island would be covered like this, intricate networks of roads leading into each other, a bloodstream to carry all the trees to the main harbour where the logs were loaded and shipped to California and Japan. They smoked another cigarette and by the time they were finished they had come out to the clearing where the old logging camp had been, nothing left of it now but the old dining hall and the building where they had kept the explosives. Parked next to the dining hall were some old machines, stiff with rust. Beyond them, was a newer bright yellow machine, a caterpillar.

Johnny had stopped and was watching Laurel while she surveyed the camp. He had taken the canvas bag off his shoulder and set it on the ground.

"See?" Johnny said. "They've been working here for two weeks. Going to go back in towards the village." The Indian Village, he meant, long abandoned. He had taken her there once. It was the only site not on the sea. It was beside an inland lake, at a place where a stream fed into it. There were still mortuary poles at the village, poles on which they had placed the coffins of the dead. Only once had they buried someone in the ground. That was Johnny Tulip's father, buried there long after anyone remembered how to carve the poles. The old camp had been only a few miles from the village, but the loggers in those days had all been Indians, and the company had agreed not to go in that direction.

"What can you do?" Johnny asked.

Laurel took the flashlight from Johnny, went to the explosives shack and shone it on the door. It was broken already, chopped away with an axe. Inside the shack had been lined with concrete blocks, all newly whitewashed. Otherwise it was empty.

"I think they're nervous," Johnny said. "In the old days there would have been lots of dynamite."

Johnny was standing outside. They inspected the yellow caterpillar tractor. It was the kind that needed keys to start. The lock was empty.

"I have the keys," Johnny said. "But there's nowhere to hide it."

"We could drive it into the lake."

"Too noisy."

Laurel shone the light until she found the gascap. "We could throw a match down here and run," she said. She laughed.

"Sure. I'll run, you throw the match. Come on." She followed him to the edge of the clearing and they began collecting dead branches. It hadn't rained for three days and the wood was almost dry. They piled the branches all around the tractor, getting armload after armload. Laurel took the gascap off and stuck a branch down into the tank. They put branches everywhere: into the steel treads of the tractor, in and around the motor, even on the steering wheel and seat. By the time they were finished the machine was completely covered, wood woven through every available hole.

"There," Laurel said. She stood back and shone the light. Piled high and surrounded by wood the tractor was a shadow-monster, a huge, improbably dense wooden structure with no conceivable explanation. Johnny got the canvas bag he had been carrying. He opened it up and pulled out a metal tin, a tin of kerosene. Johnny spilled the kerosene carefully over the bottom pieces, soaked the branch leading into the gastank.

He stood back with Laurel and they surveyed what they had done. There was a sudden noise from the edge of the clearing and Laurel swung the light. Two golden-green eyes, it was that doe again, she was sure. Its eyes were caught by the light. Then it turned away, immune already.

"You see," Johnny said. "She likes you."

76

"Sure," Laurel said. "If I had my gun, I'd shoot it." She dug into her pocket for the matches, lit one and held it to the wood. For a second nothing happened. Then the kerosene caught, jumping all around the tractor so quickly that they were startled into running. Laurel saw the doe's eyes again as they ran towards the bush, illuminated by the fire, grown large again, green-gold saucers splitting apart in the light. She shouted as she approached it, clapping her hands and trying to scare it into the bush. Finally it bolted, just as they were a few feet away, and the explosion came seconds later, when they were protected only by the first few trees. It was much more than she had expected, the whole clearing lit up, debris flying everywhere. She kept running and then turned to look again. Johnny was no longer with her. She worked her way back to the clearing. The fire was dying. The kerosene had all burned with a flash and left the wood as it was, half-wet and just covered with a few unsuccessful sparks.

"Johnny," Laurel whispered. She suddenly thought he might be lying somewhere, dead or fatally injured, pierced by flying pieces of the tractor. "Johnny?"

"Goddamn," Johnny said. "I knew this would happen."

"What?"

The flashlight went on. He was walking around the edge of the clearing, pointing the light at the ground.

"I lost my bag," Johnny said. He turned the light towards the tractor. The wood had all blown off it and was lying on the ground. The tractor was exactly as it was, except that where the gas tank and motor used to be there was a big hole.

She stumbled and bent over. "Here it is," she said. "Let's get going." The noise from the explosion had been so loud that her voice and Johnny's barely penetrated the sound that was still reverberating in her skull.

They were at the paved road before Johnny shone the

light on his arm. His jacket and shirt had been slashed open and there was a long cut running from his elbow to his wrist. He held the light closer and they could see the cut was only shallow, the skin smooth and wet with blood, struggling to put itself back together. "You shouldn't have hid the bottle," Laurel said.

They found a stream and Laurel splashed his arm with water, rust-brown. The flashlight was growing dimmer and the moon was now covered with more layers of clouds, passing in and out of view with the wind.

"They won't go in there for days," Laurel said. "It's going to rain all week." She tore a piece off the bottom of Johnny's shirt and wrapped it around his arm. "You see," she said, "I took first aid in school."

Johnny held his arm above his head and they started to walk again.

"It's not a bad cut," Laurel said. "You'll be able to play tonight."

"Sure," Johnny said.

When they finally got back to the cabin it was early morning and it had started to rain, the wind sweeping up the beach from the south, pushing them as they walked, driving the rain onto their shoulders and backs. Calvin was awake, drinking tea and reading by the light of a kerosene lamp. When they came in the door he stood up, put on his coat and went out without speaking.

Six

He knew that he had slipped away from his past, eluded it in some secret and final way. And on certain afternoons, while he sat in his office and watched the rain falling endlessly into the parking lot of his hotel, C.W. Smith would try to locate the exact moment when this mysterious and necessary separation had occurred. But although he had memories, they were not very many, and the event seemed to have receded deep into a childhood he could hardly recall. It was true that Mary Gail told him that some nights he sat straight up in bed and talked so loud and so fast she was woken up by the noise. Perhaps this was supposed to be evidence of another life struggling to be lived. It was a possibility he could hold carefully in his mind and consider while looking out the window—and then discard as soon as it was time to drink or tend the bar.

He had grown accustomed to his body, and now he almost liked it. When it was newer it had been awkward and chaotic, the flesh jumping nervously to every touch. But the Montana sun had finally dried it out and cured it, turned it into something that could be trusted. His wife had said to him that he was like a fence post with a pot belly. When he moved to the island and bought the hotel he switched from beer to liquor, and his belly melted away, the rain accomplishing what the sun could never do.

When he had come back from the war he had spent long afternoons at the movies, and longer evenings parked in front of the television set at the house of his parents. Now, instead, he rented a room in his own hotel. And although, on the dresser, he had a colour television, he didn't need to watch it anymore.

Even when he looked at himself in the mirror, he saw old movies. Letting his eyes drop slightly out of focus, standing in the middle of the false yellow light of his room, he could see himself as he really was: tall and contained, almost as stately as an ambassador. And moving closer so he saw only his head, he would ritualistically tap his skull with his knuckles, as if prepared to discover he had long been inhabiting a black-haired melon that had now grown hollow.

Not only did he shave in the morning, every morning, from the short sideburns that ended near the middle of his ears right down to the collarbone, but he also did exercises. He had been in the airforce and he still did the same routine he had done then: touching his toes with alternate hands, fifty pushups and fifty situps. And, standing in front of the mirror, wearing his striped pants and his undershirt, he would brace his hands against his waist and bend in all directions, his torso a gun rotating from the turret of his hips.

One morning he sat in the dark room of the closed bar and talked with the government men. "C.W.," they called him, the initials sliding out like long chains of dollar bills. They sat in the bar and they asked him how easy it would be to cut new logging roads into the forest and he answered that it would be very easy indeed, as easy as driving from one end of the island to the other in a hearse, a riddle none of them solved until that night when they went down to meet the barge and get their official government mail. And, right behind the battered red government truck that delivered the mail from the mainland, was a brand new hearse—complete with flags, cellophane on the leather seats, a colour television that folded down into the back, and a silver avenging angel.

"An old family habit," C.W. explained. The mark of prosperity that carried with it the preparation for that long ignorant sleep which he knew himself to fear so much that this year he had stopped taking out life insurance, preferring to bet on his immortality rather than his death.

C.W. loved riddles. He knew, for example, all of the ten commandments, the only person on the island who could recite them except for Johnny Tulip and, it was rumoured, the minister's wife. C.W. was also the only person who knew of a certain Russian composer who drank in the mornings. Like all communists he drank vodka exclusively, and that to excess.

C.W. drove the government men up and down the island in the hearse. But when he went in the next day to show them the roads, wading through the muck in raingear and waist-high wading boots for the men from Ottawa and Victoria, he found that his new caterpillar tractor had had the motor blown out of it.

"Is there a problem here?" the man from Ottawa had asked.

"Oh no," C.W. said, twisting his mouth around the Montana vowels. The government man wasn't looking at the machine, but the door of the explosives shack, which had been reduced to firewood, splintered to new edges very fresh and red and unweathered, by an axe that was buried in the remains.

"You know how it is on Saturday nights," C.W. said. "We were going to burn this place down anyway."

There was a dining room in the hotel. It had never

been used but now, for the government men, C.W. opened it up. He had read somewhere that Canadians eat hot beef sandwiches for lunch, so that is what he served them. The meat and bread were covered by an instant gravy he himself had prepared the night before. And Mary Gail surrounded each plate with green canned peas and fried potatoes.

C.W. watched Mary Gail as she arranged the food with the same bland confidence she did everything else. There were even times in the short intense nights of this northern summer that she had broken him open, sent him half-running out of his own room in his own hotel into the cold gravel streets of this logging town, as if nothing else mattered except getting through to the morning. And although he had reduced his family to photographs and postcards, Mary Gail was bathed in hers, her dead father and sister, her crazy dying brother who insisted on coming every night and pounding the piano to death, and most of all her mother, who seemed ecstatically blind, who came to the lounge occasionally and sat in the very middle, listening to the piano and holding court with all around her, her face permanently marked by a grin as wide as an axe.

Standing beside the ruined tractor C.W. had shifted his weight from one foot to the other, trying to ease the hurt he felt in his hips and legbones in the rain. Sometimes he thought he was getting rheumatism and could imagine himself confined to the lobby of his hotel, at first limping with a cane and finally reduced to a wheelchair. But the memory of his wedding night had escaped him almost completely. He knew only that they had gone to a hotel and that he had gotten change for a twenty dollar bill.

His wife had started keeping long-haired cats. Now he sent her money and she sent him pictures of the cats winning prizes, standing on tables with her hands holding them firmly, curled asleep in their special cushion she used for these pictures, placed on the dining-room table where they would be warmed by the light of the whole southern hemisphere, the flat Montana plain pouring in everything.

When he came back for lunch with the government men, there was a boy waiting for him in the dining room. The boy had thick black hair and olive skin. He had a name that C.W. was able to forget as quickly as he said it, a foreign name that the boy pronouned in its own way, the words not only unrepeatable but impossible even to properly hear.

"Pleased to meet you," C.W. had finally said. The boy's head was marked by burns where the hair met his skin. His hands were the hands of a mechanic, small cuts blackened with grease and oil.

"I drove your hearse for you," the boy said.

"Thanks." C.W. walked with him towards the side of the room, away from the table with the white tablecloth and silver.

"I just wanted to meet you," the boy said. "Again, I mean." C.W.'s hand was extended. The boy met it with his own, C.W.'s palm against his feeling tough and dry, feeling as he had looked while the barge floated slowly in to be docked, a tall bony man in a vest whom the boy had seen waiting on the shore as the barge drew near, watching the hearse so closely that the boy knew right away that it was his, could imagine this thin half-visible man cutting out an advertisement of the silver angel and holding it in his hand, as if it might come alive. And as soon as the barge was fastened to the dock of the island C.W. had jumped up onto the metal deck, dove into the front seat of the hearse and drove it to where the men were waiting for him. Leaving the boy to make his own way to the hotel, the island as strange and impenetrable beneath his feet as it had been in his dreams. And looking back before he left the dock the boy tried to see the mainland. But nothing at all was visible, only a clear sky and endless broken ranks of rolling waves.

"You hungry?" C.W. asked. "You can have a sandwich."

The boy looked automatically to the kitchen. And then to the three government men sitting at the table, gradually emptying their plates.

"I've eaten," the boy said. He held his hands in front of him. He had been on the island less than a day. But the night and the morning of rain had already made it seem familiar to him, a warning too late to be useful.

"I picked up hitch-hikers," the boy said. "You know how it is. I had to drive all the way in seven days. It's over three thousand miles."

"Sure," C.W. said. He signalled to Mary Gail. As she passed him, C.W. patted her. He looked back to the boy. He saw the boy's eyes following her.

"When I got to Vancouver, they told me I could deliver it here," the boy said. "It's really a beautiful place." He smiled at C.W. as he spoke. He wore a black moustache that was silky and smooth. He held his hand folded in front of him, the cuts blackened by oil, but the skin young and veinless.

"You looking for a job?"

"No," the boy said. "I guess I'm just moving around. You know." He had spent the night in an old shed behind the hotel. In the morning Mary Gail had discovered him.

"Well," C.W. said. "Here's five dollars." He reached into his back pocket for his wallet.

"No thanks."

But by the time the boy had spoken, C.W. had his wallet out. He saw the boy glance at it and then turn his eyes towards Mary Gail.

"You handy?"

"What?"

"Can you fix things?"

"Sure," the boy said. "I guess." His eyes were large and

brown. They never looked at C.W. but only at different parts of the room, at Mary Gail, at the men eating their hot beef sandwiches.

"I guess I could use a mechanic," C.W. said. "Someone to take care of big machines."

"I like to drive," the boy said.

"I could pay you three dollars an hour," C.W. said. "You want a sandwich?"

"No thanks," the boy said. "I had one."

C.W. was still holding his wallet out. He folded it up and shoved it back in his pocket.

"Okay," the boy said. "See you later."

By the time C.W. sat down at the table, one of the government men had already finished eating. It was their last day on the island. They had inspected everything and had told C.W. the timber lease would be granted. Now they were just sight-seeing until it was time to take the ferry. The man who was smoking let his ashes drop casually in the unfinished remains of his meal, the uneaten gravy gathered together into a small dead volcano that now received these ashes and, finally, the butt of the cigarette, twisted into the lump of gravy and bread, broken sideways at the filter.

C.W. wrapped his hand around a small glass of grapefruit juice, tipped it back, noticed how cloudy and sour the juice was—and suddenly remembered a dream. In the dream he was running through a field, his hands held to his ears, running to escape a dog falling from the sky.

When he was young his eyes had always focused and his reflexes were quick and nervous. But when he went into the airforce they wouldn't let him be a pilot. They made him a gunner instead. Every time before the plane went up he would crawl down the narrow fusilage to his position, encased rigidly in a glass bubble where he would sweep the sky for enemy fighters, his gun rotating with his eyes.

At first he was so scared that when they came back from

a mission he would feel as if he was being reborn, crawling back out the narrow tunnel to the air and a place where he could stand and move about.

In the dream there was no escape and the field was endless in all directions.

As he put down the glass, Mary Gail was standing beside him. She had one hand on his shoulder and was setting the plate down on the table.

"Do you want your coffee now?"

"Sure." The plate had somehow tipped, and gravy was running onto the paper place mat.

The government men nodded too. Except for one, a younger man whose grey suit was flecked with brown and had wide lapels and an extra button.

He was so inconspicuous that C.W. realized that he had hardly noticed him the whole time. "I'll have tea," the man said. He smiled at Mary Gail. "I hope it's no extra trouble."

"No."

He couldn't remember how the dream ended. There must have been some sort of explosion when the dog hit the ground. Maybe he had been killed in the dream, and that was why he couldn't remember.

In the war he had been afraid of dying in the bomber. But mostly he had been afraid that they would be forced down and he would be captured. In the end, they would have him lined up against the wall. He would not be the only person waiting to be shot, but, in fact, one of a long line, a line so long that the victims outnumbered the executioners. So they would be blindfolded but there would be no roll of drums, last cigarette, chaplain kneeling by the body for the final rites. Instead there would be a few soldiers sweeping the wall with machine guns. And a long row of puppets falling idiotically to the ground, out of control, arms flailing against the broken bricks in one last hopeless gesture.

If Mary Gail was with him when he woke up, he made her go to her own room. He had always hated his wife walking in on him when he was doing his exercises. But even more he had disliked her long-haired cats. They shed their fur everywhere, moulting at the slightest excuse, their only reaction to heat, or cold, to a change of season or feeling. He never liked the look of them but bald they were an insult not only to all living things but to God Himself, Whose Presence C.W. had never found consistent with anything else he saw, and therefore ruled ordinarily impossible.

After dark Mary Gail was explosive with heat. Her body beneath the sheets was like a furnace gone out of control and when he was going to spend the night with her he would open the windows and throw the blankets on the floor.

Her great warmth was famous to her family as well as her lovers; and her brother, Johnny Tulip, had said once that when it got coldest in winter they all fought to share her bed.

One after the other, the government men looked at their watches. When they were walking in the bush and forest they puffed out quickly. They preferred the tours made by helicopter, flying around the area to be inspected in slow circles while C.W., piloting and talking at once, handed out cigarettes and described what they were seeing.

Altogether there were three of them. Two from Victoria and one, the youngest, from the federal government in Ottawa. Now he coughed and looked around the table, to see if it was all right that he spoke. His clothes were different and more expensive. His hair was sandy brown, darker than his eyebrows which were almost albino blond and thin, so pale that they would have been invisible had his skin not been even whiter.

"The tractor," he said.

"Yes."

"I wanted to know if the tractor had been sabotaged," the young man said. He looked very concerned and earnest. When they had driven up and down the island with Mary Gail he had sat in the very front seat of the hearse, obviously horrified, drinking as fast as C.W. would hand him the bottle. C.W. was sure that he had been sick as soon as he got back to the hotel. Or perhaps he had written postcards late into the night.

"I guess it was damaged," C.W. said.

"But, would you think it was intentional?"

"Well," C.W. said, "I don't think it fucked itself to death." The two older men laughed with him.

Now C.W. also looked at his watch. In a few minutes it would be time for him to drive the men over to the other side of town, for their final meeting with the management of the logging company.

"I thought," the young man said, "that perhaps the incident with the tractor was a symptom of the problems you and the company had with the native population." As he said this Mary Gail slid his cup of tea in front of him. He waited until she had gone to continue. "You know," he said, "the Indians."

"Sure," C.W. said. "Everything's fine. Look at Mary Gail. She could have scalped you right there."

One of the other government men pushed his plate away and stood up. They all stood up. "It's been a pleasure meeting you," the young man said. He extended his arm across the table, the wrist shooting out of his four-button jacket, pale and thin, wrapped round by a gold watch band.

"My pleasure," C.W. said.

"There will be a letter from the minister," one of the older men said. "And when there's an announcement, there will be reporters."

"We'll be ready," C.W. said. These civil servants from

Victoria sounded almost like Englishmen with their soft, careful voices.

"I guess the company can handle them," the older man said.

"That's right," C.W. said. "I just serve the drinks."

They had walked out from the dining room, through the lobby to the front of the hotel. After the days of sun the island had settled back into the usual rain. There was an awning spread out under the HOTEL sign. A wooden sidewalk ran in front of the hotel.

The street had been widened and dug out in preparation for paving. Now it was filled with gravel, waiting for one more dry week. They could see the big station wagon from the company making its way towards them, slowly through the wet gravel. Then the driver, seeing them, accelerated, sending gravel spraying behind the wheels. He skidded to a stop in front of the hotel.

"I started right away," the boy said. He grinned. His teeth were milky white beneath his black moustache, white and large like a child's teeth. He saw the men waiting and jumped out of the station wagon, held the doors open for them.

"I put the hearse around the back," the boy said. "In the garage."

"Sure."

"Something like that should last forever," the boy said. "You know, like a Rolls Royce." The government men were settled and the boy got back in the car, rolled up his window.

"Be sure to come up in the summer," C.W. said to the government men. The rain was blown momentarily by the wind. He felt unpleasantly exposed. He turned around and went back into the hotel, the station wagon moving away before the door had closed behind him.

He had an office in the hotel and he went there now, closing the door behind him. The office was as cluttered as his room was empty. In the cupboard were piled raingear and hunting clothes. Three rifles too were shoved in the corner. One, a present from his wife's brother, was a .325 magnum that he had never even shot. His own rifle, the one he always used, was a .270. Enough to kill anything on this island, without tearing it apart and ruining the trophy. He also had a .22. He had bought it one day in Vancouver for something to do.

C.W.'s desk was covered with the papers and bills that needed to be totalled up and paid every month. There was a teacher who did this for him, he himself couldn't stand to do it. Even when he had been running his business in Montana he had hired someone to come in every month and do the accounts.

He had bought his desk, along with most of the rest of the furniture in the hotel, in a lot, in Vancouver. He had an office chair that tilted and rolled along the floor on brass castors.

In the dream he had been running away from the falling dog, through an endless field. The field reminded him somehow of those places in Montana where it was so flat that the horizon was perfectly circular. But he couldn't really picture them anymore, nor could he really see the edges of the field in his dream.

His feet felt cold and damp. Now he remembered that in the dream he had been cold too. He closed his eyes and tried to revive the exact image. He didn't see anything at all, recalled instead the feeling of running over the rough ground, his body jolting with every step, ankles and knees twisting on this soil which had been ploughed but not harrowed, clumps of earth frozen and bombed into place. The field seemed without boundary although sometimes there was a hint of trees in the distance. The night raids had been indistinct too, only the tracer bullets and the fires visible, lighting up the clouds of smoke that rose from the cities they were destroying.

When they came back the last time he had crawled down the fusilage feeling obliviously happy, rested even, so happy he had slept on the way back. He staggered out of the plane and there were newsmen there, lined up to take the pictures of the pilot and the crew. The cameras flashed over and over, so soon and so quickly there was no time to ask if everyone else had gotten back. And he had still felt drowsy and happy, only gradually aware that everyone was beginning to centre on him. And suddenly he felt his warmth was wet too, looked down at his crotch and saw his flying suit soaked bright red with blood. He fainted and when he woke up in the infirmary was afraid for hours to look down or feel with his hands.

After that he couldn't go back in the airplane at all. He had been afraid of the firing squad. Now he dreamed of it every night, his soul inhabiting each body in turn as the long line of men fell forward from the brick wall. But in the day, with the sun coming through the windows of this hospital with its thick stone walls, that same irrelevant dopey happiness that had come upon him in the air filled him until he thought he would burst apart and cry.

When the sun had just disappeared and it was twilight he would sit in the lounge and look out at the fields, pink and gold, so old, all of Europe so old and dead that they had ploughed the fields and only planted them with bombs and frost, so old they had brought in the Americans to complete their own destruction. And, when the sun was no longer visible but the light was still spread across the earth, he knew what he had been seeing from the air was not only fire and clouds but something being cut away from beneath him. "Montana is everything there is," his father had told him, as his last advice before he went to war. And when both sun and light were gone it was true. He would make his way back from the lounge to the long ward where he and the others would play cards until it was time to sleep. And in between sorting his hand and counting points he would start to prepare for his dreams, his hands and feet sweating, facing these stiff foreign soldiers with their stolen machine guns and words he had never known.

Seven

In his mother's house the night was quiet. Johnny Tulip could hear the breathing of the old woman, hoarse but strong, asleep in her living-room chair. His arm was still sore but, as Laurel had said, he had been able to play. He sat by the window in the room of his sister, Victoria. The wind moved easily through the empty space, like a sleepy cat it puffed against the cold door, threatened to collapse at every moment. From this room he could see the harbour, the water calm and flat in this clear moment of the night, holding the moon white and full in its belly. The government men had left already, flown away in the afternoon. Soon they would be back. Not them, but others like them, more of them, ready to measure the trees into newspapers and houses, luxury toothpicks for the mainland.

He could feel the urge to cough building up in his throat, held it there while his hand swung out and captured the half-empty bottle of wine from the windowsill. A strange white wine that Mary Gail had stolen for him from the hotel, a bottle with an elaborate label and a smell that was delicate and musty.

The cough was not fooled; it forced its way up, spraying through the liquid in his throat. Johnny coughed, then coughed again, hammering his hand into his chest to force it all out, then taking another swallow to wash it down.

Victoria's clothes, six years old, were still as she had left them, draped over an old three-legged chair in the corner, hung up to dry near the stovepipe, stuffed into an unpainted oak bureau the minister had brought from the mainland. They had buried her in the same clothes she drowned in, a pair of jeans and a maroon sweater the old woman had knit for her. The next afternoon Johnny had come up to her room, intending to clean it up and throw out whatever no one wanted.

This night was maybe the hundredth time he had intended to finally do it, rid the house of this old ghost it shouldn't have to contain. But now the dust and the habit of the room had made it impossible. Johnny had covered her bed with his sleeping bag. Even to begin to sort out her things and put them away in the cardboard boxes he had long ago piled in the corner for this very purpose, he would first have to move the accumulation of his own clothes and newspapers and pocketbooks, the coleman stove that he had placed on top of her trunk, the various knives and axes and about-to-be-repaired kerosene lamps that constituted his particular preserve in this household. Also the diary from the last-but-one minister's wife was hidden somewhere here, Victoria's room being the only place in the house that was his alone, no one but him having even stepped inside since the day she was buried.

Periodically he could hear the wicker chair creak as the old woman shifted in her sleep. Last winter he had been afraid she would die in the night, that he would come down one morning to find her stiff and cold in that same chair she seemed to live and sleep in almost all the time. But now he knew she would outlive him, that it would be she who would wake up one morning and know without question that he was somewhere dead, perhaps even upstairs, and would tell Mary Gail to go and arrange what was necessary.

It was not long since he had come home from the lounge, leaving even before it closed tonight, walking stiffly through the wet streets with his bottle of wine and sore arm, then stopping in front of his house to piss one last time before climbing the stairs of the porch, tiptoeing past his already sleeping mother and up the steep old stairs to Victoria's room.

He reached into his pocket, to find the candle he had taken from the kitchen. This jacket was new, or at least different, a blue-black serge jacket from Harry Jones's infinite supply to replace the one that had been torn in the explosion last night. This one had all its pockets still intact. In one of them he had found a yellowed ferry ticket, both departure and destination erased by age. He set the candle on the sill beside the bottle, and started searching around in the pockets again, this time for tobacco and papers.

"Johnny. Johnny." At first he thought he had dreamed the voice but then as he woke up he heard it a second time, cutting through the remains of the night, pulling him up now in Victoria's bed, sending him stumbling forward to stand at the head of the stairs. Mary Gail's door was open. The moon, high now, illuminated the floor of her empty room. She would be at the hotel now, drunk and asleep in C.W.'s bed. It seemed she only came home now when they had been fighting, carrying her bruises like luggage.

His mother's breathing had returned to normal, a dull saw laboriously working its way through the night. He went back to Victoria's room and got the candle. Then went downstairs and lit it. His mother was lying on the floor, head cradled in her arms, asleep. In the old days she could walk seriously in her sleep, walk out of the house and down the road to the cove where her husband had once kept a boat. She would find a place to sit by the sea until she got woken by the morning or the tide. Then, helplessly, wait for someone to come to get her.

Now her ambitions had lessened. Some nights she tried to move from the chair to the old couch that was only a few steps away. Johnny bent down to pick her up. She was beginning to stink in her old age. But not to rot: she was still almost too heavy for him to lift, and after he finally got her to the couch he had to go to the kitchen to wipe the new blood from his cut.

When Victoria was alive she would wake up without being called. They would come back from the cove carrying a huge basket of mussels, the morning still new and the mist hanging in the air expectantly, waiting to be shattered by the sun.

The house was growing cold and damp. Soon he would have to stay at home at nights, tend the fire so his mother wouldn't freeze. Before Victoria died the memory of her sight had kept her going. She had moved about the house with perfect confidence, ministering to the stove and the garden as if they were attached to her nerves.

He still had the candle from the living-room. He held it to the wick of a lantern and then, as he lowered the mantle, the kitchen jumped into its night-time existence, the walls covered with old photographs and wood smoke, wavering in the uncertain light of the lantern, the stove looming a vast black shadow at the back of the room. His mother groaned and her breathing deepened into long hoarse sighs. Johnny found paper and kindling and started a fire, building it until the noise of the burning drowned out the noise from the next room. The fire caught slowly these days; the pipes too old and rusty to survive another cleaning—they would need to be replaced before the snow.

Tonight his chest was miraculously calm. Suspended

between seasons, or at least soothed by the sight of the exploding tractor, he felt curiously renewed, a brief flash of how it had once been to spend weeks alone on the coast, fishing during the day and sleeping away the long nights in Harry Jones's old army tent, the canvas thick and heavy, never yielding to the rain. In those times when he was up in the middle of the night he would walk down to the ocean and let himself float like a dead man in the water, letting the cold jump up between his legs, wrap around and try to find its way inside him. Float like a dead man in the water, the salt holding him up and the slow rain beating down on his belly and chest until finally it was so strange he would swim by sliding beneath the surface of the water in long steady strokes, wishing he could sprout gills and swim this way forever, breathing out long chains of bubbles from his nose, like a weed with an unexpected flower.

And the water and the cold would finally work its way in and around him, shrinking his skin and his flesh, pressing it tight against his bones so he became smooth and taut and slippery, an eel sliding through the waters, grounding belly-down on the sharp cold sand, flopping and wriggling into shore, frozen and shivering, ready to build a huge fire and slap his skin back into existence, slapping his wet palms against his skin until it hurt, drawing out the blood from the centre of his belly so he could be warm again.

Johnny stood in the doorway between the kitchen and the living-room. In one hand he held a huge mug of steaming tea. In the other, the candle. As he passed through the room to the stairs he bent over to check on his mother. She had slid from the couch to the floor, without waking, and was as he had first found her, her head tucked into her arms. Nothing could wake her between midnight and sunrise; even when Mary Gail was an infant Victoria was the one who had to get up with her, and shove her to the breast where she fed contentedly on her sleeping mother. He set the mug and the candle on the first stair and then bent over her again. Now that her breathing was so long and hoarse it seemed she uttered his name with every sigh, groaned it out as he wrestled her up on the couch again, covering her again with the quilt she always used, an old flame-red quilt the minister's wife had given her after Victoria drowned.

At the window again in Victoria's room, he sipped his tea slowly, letting the steam swell up around his face. He drank his tea with sugar and canned milk, the way Victoria used to make it for him, the way Laurel Hobson made it for him too. So like Victoria that when they stood above her drowned body on the beach, her skin whitened by the water and cold, he had looked back and forth from Laurel to Victoria as if the existence of the one would have to revive the other. And his skin still wet with Laurel's sweat, his pants sticking to him, where he had stuck to her. And the first thing that he thought, while Laurel was already crying over Victoria, was that now she would be his, that this death had been fated, to seal them together.

"We'll have to go to the village," he said finally. "I don't want to carry her like this."

"You knew," Laurel said. She had stepped up to him and grabbed his shirt as if to choke him, her fists digging into his neck.

"No."

"Yes," she insisted, "you knew the whole time." Her face red and contorted, looking not like Victoria at all any more, angrier than Victoria had ever been. But after that she was quiet, letting him lead her up the beach to the village, not crying though her face stayed red. And the next day, when they brought Victoria back, Laurel stood with the family as they buried her, not crying, small and passive.

Right after the funeral Laurel had insisted on going back up the beach to her cabin. And he had followed her, not knowing how to argue with her, sliding after Laurel down the small sand cliff where she had hurt herself that spring, following her to her cabin where she opened the door and they both saw the partly-full bottle of birthday wine he had brought with him, the wine his brother had given him. But Victoria, who had died on his birthday, now stood implacably between them. And even before Laurel had time to turn and talk to him, he was gone from her cabin, the bottle of wine left on the rough plank floor, his belt suddenly heavy with the new knife his brother had given him, the knife his brother had waved in the air before Johnny, saying now the world was cut in two.

The sound of the iron skillet banging on the top of the kitchen stove woke him up, iron against iron, and Mary Gail talking as she worked, bits of gossip about the hotel floating through the grey morning air. Soon it would start to snow. His mother had said there would be a lot of snow this winter. If the snow was deep it would slow down the loggers, they would have to finish building their roads in the spring. Still wearing his jacket he rolled onto his back and then sat up. He rubbed his teeth with his fingers and then started his first cigarette of the day, the smoke soaking into him as he stood by Victoria's old window and surveyed what he could see of the harbour through the mist and the cloud. When his back was stretched and he had slid into his shoes, he made his way downstairs, the cigarette out but still clamped firmly between his teeth, ready to be lit again when he started the cup of coffee he could already smell.

Mary Gail had no new bruises. Only a big bag of groceries that sat like a trophy on the table, surrounded by the plates and the cutlery she had already put out for breakfast.

When Victoria died she had refused to look at the body, spent days after in her room, the furniture jammed up against the door.

"Up early this morning," his mother said. She was sitting in the kitchen, near the stove, her perpetual knitting in her hands and lap.

Johnny looked automatically for the clock that had once been there, when Mary Gail was still going to school.

"You have to get up early in the morning," his mother said.

"Just in time for breakfast," Mary Gail said. She stepped forward from the stove, her cheeks flushed and radiant from the heat. She threw her arms around Johnny's neck and hugged him, making him lose his balance so they both stumbled and collapsed against the table, bumping against their mother.

"Can't even stand up anymore," the old woman said sharply.

"She's getting mean in the morning," Mary Gail said. "You have to watch your step in the morning."

"Your father was worse," the old woman said. She had resumed the rhythm of her knitting, the wooden needles clicking softly against the sounds of the fire.

Johnny poured himself coffee from the stove while Mary Gail laid strips of bacon in the skillet, each one bubbling and hissing as it was put into the boiling fat. His mother's eyes were closed and her mouth was set.

Eight

The smoke seemed to have frozen in Calvin's throat, his whole body suddenly immobilized in time, stuck, turning to wood as the chemicals seeped from the smoke into his blood. The light from the kerosene lamp was distant and white. It pushed back the white walls of their cabin, bringing close only the black rectangles of doors. There was something in the pale quality of the light that was cruel, declared the space between them as they moved back and forth in the cabin, performing the small evening tasks of maintenance that had already become unquestioned ritual.

Then he exhaled, pulling his stomach in and with it the cold light from the room, drawing it in to the centre of his belly as he blew out the smoke. As he did the room seemed to soften. Laurel swam into focus, sitting across from him on the couch, her hand stretched out to receive, as Johnny Tulip called it, Mother's Best, rolled this time in chocolate papers that Calvin had found in the gift shop.

"Thank you," Laurel said, smiling. Her words seemed to him not merely formal but a subtle elaboration on his own formality, a comment on the way he had passed it to her, careful not to burn or touch her fingers.

Even while she was drawing in the smoke she kept her

eyes on him, letting them expand as she inhaled, an expansion of her own statement which he started to follow but then lost as his attention jumped to the wind which she created as she sucked in, mixing with the sound of the burning wood, the slow rain that had been falling for days now, gradually closing them in towards winter.

"Were you ever in love with Johnny Tulip?" Calvin asked.

"What?"

"Nothing." With his question he had already convinced himself that there was something peculiar about these long rainy evenings, in which they stalked each other warily, from the beginning of supper until the moment when fatigue and the boredom with being inside pushed Laurel into yawning and asking him to make some tea.

"Did you ask me if I was in love with Johnny Tulip?"

"I guess so," Calvin said. Now that she had said it instead of him, it sounded unlikely, even impossible. Or perhaps there was something tragic and unspeakable, a reason why they weren't together.

"Maybe you're in love with Johnny Tulip."

"Me?"

"Sure," Laurel said. She leaned towards him, passing back the Mother's Best. The paper was supposed to be chocolate but the truth was that although it was dark and faintly sweet, he could neither smell nor taste it.

"I like the imitation dollar bills better," Calvin said. Then inhaled again, this time pulling the smoke in as deep as he could, down into his lungs and further, so he could feel it spreading through his belly, blotting out everything except the sudden sensation of his refuelled blood whirling madly through his arms and legs and guts.

Laurel crossed her arms and hunched over, her elbows on her knees, rocking back and forth, her brown eyes wide open and observing him closely. And again Calvin felt stiff and wooden, more frozen than the light of the room which had caught them now in this pose, fixed the stares and smiles that echoed back and forth between them, suspended.

"What are you thinking?"

"Oh," Calvin said. "Sometimes I wonder where I am."

"Where are you?"

"Here." And saw his body locked into the chair, his legs crossed, one hand resting on the chair and the other pushing the chocolate-coloured cigarette into the space between them.

"Oh really," Laurel said, leaning forward too, reaching out her hand so it too moved through the frozen space, moving slowly, a boat rowing upstream.

"I mean," she said. "Do you ever?" She stopped and laughed, her voice sending spirals of colour through the air. She took the cigarette.

"All the time," Calvin said. Laurel had got up and was looking in the wood stove. The firebox opened and was filled by the red glow of the ashes.

"I'll get some wood," Calvin said. He felt frozen still, his body stiff and inevitable as a robot's. Standing up in a thousand tiny clashing motions. Then brushing his hands together and pulling up his sleeves. The weeks on the island had changed his arms, made them stringy with muscles and scrapes where they had been round and smooth.

"Okay," Laurel said. And as he passed her on the way to the door her hand flared fast and warm onto his back, leaving again before he could turn.

In the rain his belly broke apart, doubled him over with pain as he reached for the axe, pain as if something had been driven into the centre of his abdomen, sharp at first and then some feeling that was neither pleasure nor hurt but only intense heat, bringing him down to his knees in the wet grass, the cold fresh air exploding in his throat and lungs. By the light that came through the windows he could see the shadows of the cedar logs that were piled untidily together in a mound. He closed his eyes and bent down further, letting his forehead rest against the wet earth. The rain hummed steadily into the ground, soaked quickly through his shirt, covering his back and neck. The water drained his body, circled his waist and diffused the heat in his stomach, letting it out. He stood up and took the axe in his hand. The wood pushed directly against the bones, as if his skin and muscle had finally lost the capacity to shelter them.

The wind seemed a live presence, curling and snapping through the rain. Selecting the logs he placed them carefully in a half-circle, between himself and the light from the cabin. And then began to split them, in order, swinging the axe carefully into the rain and the shadows, letting it crack the wood by its own weight.

When he came back in Laurel was sitting on the couch again, as close as possible to the kerosene lamp, the newspaper folded, on her lap, doing the crossword puzzle. Calvin fixed the fire and went to sit beside her. She reached out absently for him, but her attention was focused entirely on the page.

"This must be the life," Calvin said.

Laurel looked up to him, and then back to the puzzle.

"We should get married." His stomach retreated into a hollow knot. Her pencil stopped and she almost flushed, her skin flickering delicate and pink.

"What?"

"You can't beat this life," Calvin said.

"Sometimes I get so tired," Laurel said. "I don't know what's wrong with me."

"You drink too much."

"I guess so," Laurel said. She reached beside her for a cigarette. On the floor, in front of them, was the ashtray.

Calvin stood up. He felt like a school of fish, confused and swimming off in all directions.

"Maybe we shouldn't be doing this," Laurel said.

"Smoking dope?"

"Living together."

Now that she had finally said it the lump in his stomach returned, solid and dead in the centre but tense at the edges, threatening to expand and take him over altogether. He felt pushed away from everything. The white walls seemed to move back further. He went through one of the black rectangles, into the bedroom, and sat on the bed. The rain splashed against the window and for some reason he felt like he was going to cry, his throat tight and painful, blades cutting through, cutting off his breath.

The new wood he put in the fire had caught, was spitting and cracking as it heated up.

"What's wrong?"

"Nothing," Calvin said. He stretched out on the bed. The mattress was soft and the springs broken and almost useless.

"I guess I could keep you around," Laurel said.

Calvin's throat tightened. He couldn't breathe. He hit his fist against his chest, trying to force the air. He opened and closed his mouth. The feelings in his stomach and throat had joined and when he finally stood up he thought that the tension must be visible on him, sparking like an aura. He went back into the living-room and sat down beside Laurel on the couch. She had put aside her crossword puzzle and was smoking a cigarette.

"I shouldn't say things like that," Laurel said.

"Don't worry about it." On the arm of the couch was the stone he had found the day he first met Johnny Tulip, the day he had been out on the beach, looking for seals. On the beach it had been wet, and the wetness had made it look deep red. When it dried the colour was duller and revealed a smoky patch on one side, like a nebula or star cluster with arms extending round the other side. In his pocket was the fossil he always carried, the butterfly-like shell. He pulled it out and set it beside the stone. In the last few months it had begun to change. Now the markings showed through more clearly, and colours too, faint browns and reds. In one place it seemed as if it was beginning to wear away. A strange surface was revealed, like a tiny section of petrified wood.

He held the fossil in his palm. He closed his eyes. The fire cracked again and he could see the flames leaping and whitening against the cast iron, the flames and half-burned smoke hissing and blowing up the stove pipes out into the rain and night wind.

Then he felt Laurel's hand on his arm, sliding lightly onto his wrist. He turned to her but it was gone again and she was looking down at her paper. The wick of the lamp had burned down and now the light was beginning to flicker, making the white walls pulse in and out.

He was still holding the fossil. He closed his eyes again. He felt sick, strangely swaying. The tension was still jumping from his stomach to his throat, like the flames he could see behind his closed eyes, that he somehow knew Laurel was seeing too.

He wondered how the shell had come to live inside the rock, if it was not really a fossil but some prehistoric moth caught in lava that was translucent and now wearing away. He could feel Laurel's eyes on his face, sweeping his skin like spotlights. The stone warmed in his hand, seemed to flutter. Her eyes had stopped at his and he could feel her waiting, stalking him. The fire had settled down, now hummed evenly. The cedar burned hot and sweet, the smoke soaking through all their clothes and utensils, gradually growing into the room as the winter approached.

"Calvin." Her voice was coloured and wispy, drifted slowly through the room. He opened his eyes and saw, in her's, tiny reflections of the kerosene lamp. He put his hand on her leg. She was wearing corduroy pants, a pair she always wore, the cords faded and worn around the knees and seat. He wanted to move his hand away but then could feel the warmth of her flesh beneath the cotton, her leg shifting minutely towards him. There was something in the way she often looked at him when they were about to make love that sometimes put him off, a look that tried to hold him with her eyes, force him to admit something that was obscure but reluctant in him.

Through the sounds of the fire and the wind he could hear the sea. Sometimes Johnny Tulip came late at night. He found himself trying to listen for his steps, push the sounds of the night into that pattern, even looking away from Laurel towards the window where Johnny Tulip always knocked before coming in.

"I don't know why I say things like that," Laurel said. "Sometimes I just feel we've settled in like a couple of old bears, sleeping away the winter."

"I guess so," Calvin said. "I've never seen a bear except in a zoo."

"Me neither," Laurel said. "They don't have them here." She started to laugh, then looked away from him, down at her leg where his hand still rested, the tattoo floating on his skin like spilled oil. She covered his hand with her hands. She was still looking down and he noticed for the first time her eyelashes, which were dark and slightly curved. The skin around her eyes was completely smooth and unmarked. Her fingers moved nervously on his hand and wrist.

"I wish I'd met you before," she said.

"When?"

"Oh. I don't know. Five years ago."

"Five years ago," Calvin said. He had been living with a woman then too, a woman who worked as a receptionist for an eye doctor. After a couple of months she had packed her suitcase and left. Then he had gotten a postcard from her saying she had run away with the doctor.

"I just don't know if I can be with anyone now."

"You seem to be here," Calvin said.

"I don't always feel here." Laurel reached behind her for the cigarettes and matches, lit one and threw the match down at the ashtray on the floor, which she missed. Then her fingers returned to his hand and wrist. She was still looking down, her eyes almost closed.

The tension in his throat and chest and stomach had dulled, but still hurt, like a fresh wound not knowing whether it would be allowed to heal.

"Sometimes I'm just waiting to die," Laurel said. But the tips of her fingers were warm, skated on the surface of his skin.

"Don't you like being alive?"

"I don't know." She moved the cigarette, flicked it absently at the floor, returned her hand to his. "I guess it's all right," she said. "When there's something I want." She glanced at him and then looked away. Usually her eyes seemed hard and bright to him, shiny and without depth. Now that surface layer seemed to have dissolved, left them transparent and empty.

"I don't know what's wrong with me," she said. "Maybe I should have stayed down in Vancouver and married a lawyer. My girlfriend married a lawyer."

"You could still marry a lawyer," Calvin said. "You could live in a big house with a vacuum cleaner and a colour television set."

"When Louise got married I went down and was her maid of honour. She wore an off-white dress, sort of a grey-beige. It was horrible." She looked up at him again, her eyes still empty, brought her cigarette to her mouth. In the pale light of the kerosene lamp her lips were pale too, thin and bloodless.

"Louise was always afraid of Johnny Tulip," Laurel said. "I should have met you before I ever came here."

"He's all right," Calvin said. Laurel seemed to have drawn into herself. Her hands were quiet on his skin, and cold. He stood up and went over to the stove. The wood had burned quickly, and was reduced to red transparent shells, ready to crumble at a touch. He closed his eyes and the image of the embers persisted. Then they seemed to sputter and disappear. But when he opened his eyes they were still there, and collapsed only when he added wood to the fire. He had to move carefully, without bending his stomach or chest. He went and sat beside Laurel. When he closed his eyes it hurt less, diffused through his skin and through the closed place in his neck, up into his skull, which now began to feel washed with light and heat, waves pulsing with the beating of his heart.

"Louise was the first girl I knew who ever went to bed with anyone. I mean, my own age. When we were in grade ten she slept with a man because he offered her five dollars."

Calvin directed his eyes, still closed, towards Laurel. He wondered if she could feel the heat escaping from his closed lids, if she knew he could see her, her skin turned almost liquid in the intensity of his sight, liquid and so fragile that the slightest disturbance might dissolve whatever it was that held her together. The light pulsed in his skull and he opened his eyes, seeing not only Laurel but his own eyes as well, from behind, the whites brilliant and colourless as ice, the pupils swollen up to fill the whole iris.

"I really thought she was awful," Laurel said. "I never slept with anyone for years, not until I came up here."

Sometimes, despite herself, she seemed absolutely

placid and removed, as if she didn't exist at all but was only someone who housed various passing spirits. Now her skin looked darker than ever and he could see how she would look as she got older. Her face would grow even more tense, her eyes brighter, the bones that framed her eyes more prominent and she would resemble some strange bird of prey, a small and wild falcon.

She had put her cigarette out and rested her hands lightly on his leg. Her fingers were small and fine, but tough too, and strong enough to tear things open. Her nails were short now, shorter than they had been two months ago when they first met and she had left scratches on his back and shoulders.

"We had champagne at the reception," Laurel said. "We started drinking and couldn't stop until it was all gone. Louise was sick, so sick she couldn't cut the cake. Her lawyer's mother came up to ask her what was wrong and Louise had to hold her hand over her mouth until I helped her to the ladies."

She stopped and glanced briefly up at Calvin, flashing that same unsure look she had earlier, as if acknowledging that some balance between them had changed without either of them willing it. "I couldn't ever get married," she said. "It would seem so stupid."

The pain in his chest had started to ease. His throat was no longer tight. But there was a band of sensation where it had opened, and waves of light and heat still washed through his skull. When Laurel talked he could see that some of the things she was saying came out of her mouth automatically, from some sealed compartment in her brain that had nothing to do with the rest of her, that was hardly even rooted in her body but only made her lips and skin move in approximate time to the words.

"I don't know what's wrong with me," Laurel said. Her eyes stayed fastened to his. He felt caught off guard. The tension streamed through him again, hurting everywhere, even his eyes which now felt swollen and tired.

"I don't know either," Calvin said. "What does it feel like?"

"Nothing, I guess. Everything just goes away."

"Maybe we should go to bed."

"Not like this."

Calvin stood up. Laurel stood up with him. He put his arms around her. She felt limp and unresponsive. Holding her, he wondered what it would be like to leave, to go down to Vancouver for the winter. Her arm was tight around his back, her hand so warm that his shirt was damp where she pressed it. He let his breathing slow down to match hers, so their bellies pushed out and receded together. Again he felt a slight but sudden movement in her, the predator stirring in its sleep.

"I'm late," she said.

"It's not that late," Calvin said. "It just seems like a long time."

"My period," Laurel said.

He could feel himself smiling, then, appalled at himself, forced his face to be rigid.

"I haven't been sick or anything," she said. "But it's a week and I'm always right on time."

He held her without moving.

"Johnny Tulip's mother told me to come to her if there was anything wrong."

"I guess he's too young to get married," Calvin said. Laurel pushed away from him and went to the couch for a cigarette.

"I'm sorry."

"I stopped taking the pill," Laurel said.

"Maybe that's why it's late. Because you stopped."

"Maybe," Laurel said. "You don't seem very happy."

"Oh. Yes. I didn't know." He sat down beside her. With

her head bent forwards her hair fell down and masked her face, and she looked suddenly like one of those women he used to watch when he first went to school, women who seemed older and unattainable, restlessly moving around the libraries and cafeterias, too human to fit in.

"What are you going to do?"

Laurel shrugged. She looked at him and the balance swung again, crazily, its centre located in his stomach and chest. He closed his eyes. He kept wanting to smile. "I'm sorry," he said. "I can't help hoping that you are." He put his hands on her shoulders. Took them away. "Did you say you stopped taking the pill?"

"Yes."

"That's nice." He wondered what this had to do with what she had been saying earlier, whether she wanted him to leave so she could have the baby alone.

"You'll have to read books and things," she said. "If we were caught here we could never get a doctor." He had a sudden brief image of her turned into a doe, her belly swollen and ripped open, the child emerging in a bloody cocoon. He went and moved the kettle over the hot part of the stove, started looking for the candles they lit every evening when it was time to make a pot of tea and go to sleep.

"I'm not trying to trap you," Laurel said.

"I know." She had never seemed to ask anything of him before, not in this immediate way. He tried to think of something to say. He could hear Laurel making strange sounds, as if she was crying. He turned around and saw that she was holding her hand over her mouth, trying not to laugh.

He blew out the lamp. In the candlelight the walls disappeared altogether, were replaced by irregular shadows swaying and jumping with the draft. The kettle was beginning to come to a boil. He brought the pot over to the counter and then took a piece out of the top of the stove, so the kettle was exposed directly to the flame. When he poured the water the steam puffed out of the pot in large balloons of liquid smoke, hissed about his head like a motorized blanket.

They took their tea and the candle into the bedroom. Then as he was carefully sitting down on the edge of the bed, his tea in one hand and the candle in the other, she was on him, knocking the cup onto the floor and the candle too, ripping his shirt off in the blackness, scratching him. When they were finally locked together, soaked in sweat and blood and juice from her insides, as she drew him closer still he knew it had been none of these nights in the cabin, which had grown isolated and almost perfunctory, but the morning by the stream when she had killed the salmon and drawn him in so deep, like this, so deep he lost himself in her. And later with the light of the candle he came into her again. In this light everything was softer, closer, their shadows gentle and transparent, so large upon the walls they seemed like huge diffuse clouds, rising and falling in and out of each other in a slow abstract dance. And in that light her face and body were only lines and shapes, a ritual mask that drew them through the loop of the night and into their own special country where more and more it seemed they were without personality or past.

He woke up with his hand folded over her belly. The room was white and intense, as if the night had washed over into the morning. Last night, the floor had been simply cold and uncomfortable, in the morning it made his toes cramp tightly into his feet. Stuffing paper and kindling into the stove he saw that there was ice on top of the bucket, not just a paper-thin film but a layer thick enough he had to poke it hard before it broke open. And it was only then, looking out the window, that he finally realized what it was that made this morning so different: the thin scattering of snow on the ground and the trees that sent the new winter light through the cabin.

Even before the fire was going he could hear the snow melting off the roof, running down the cabin's one eavestrough into the hooped wooden barrel someone had placed carefully on a huge old stump. Strange white plants were growing from the sides of the barrel into the water, so they never used or emptied it, just left it sitting there, perpetually overflowing in the perpetual rain.

When he got back to bed Laurel had changed position, was lying flat on her stomach, hips and belly and breasts pushing into the mattress. He slid in beside her, enveloped in her heat, a vaguely sweet and milky smell that rose like vapours from her skin.

"It snowed," Calvin said. He put his hand on her back, hot, and Laurel pushed herself deeper into the mattress. The skin on her back was thin and tight, spotted irregularly with small black moles and, on her shoulders, a scattering of freckles that seemed almost childish and out of place. When she wriggled he could see the play of all her muscles. Like the deer, skinned, there would be no fat at all, only blue-grey sheets stretched and criss-crossed over each other, fastened to the bones by fine white fibres.

He fitted himself to her, slid his hand round to her stomach again, closed his eyes. He heard the sounds of different birds, outraged, protesting against the snow. With the cold weather they seemed to nest closer to the cabin, hoping for edible garbage, sending their signals back and forth across the sharp peaked roof. And every morning they sounded different to him, newly invented, the high-pitched whistles and calls carved out of each particular day.

Laurel turned towards him, hugging him to her, wrapping her arms around his neck as she turned. There was a moment when her elbow brushed past his face and he was reminded of Johnny Tulip, could feel his temper flare, push her away. She had her mouth in his neck, her tongue exploring and pushing against his skin. He wondered how she had liked being with Johnny Tulip, whether his skin was as it seemed: thick and leathery, sour to the touch and taste.

Her morning breath was sour too. He turned his head away, caressed her back and pulled her to him automatically. He slid his hands up to her neck, to the back of her skull; it was impossibly hard and rounded, the coconut skull of a monkey.

If she had the child her breasts and belly would have to change to include it, would accommodate it in a way that neither he nor Johnny Tulip could ever know or understand. She looked up at him, her eyes as blank and impermeable as her head which he still held, sliding his hands about it as if it were inanimate, a rock. He was pressed against her but then she moved and had him inside her, a mysterious trick she had, her third eye he called it once, making her blush scarlet, the only time he ever managed that with words.

"Do you like this?" Laurel asked.

"What?"

"Lying still."

"It's all right," Calvin said. "And we don't want to disturb anything."

"No," Laurel said. "I hope it didn't fall out last night."

"I suppose I'll have to meet your aunt."

"Oh yes. I wrote her about you."

"What did you say?" Holding her he couldn't tell where he ended and she began, where they ended and the bed and the air began, what noises were their breathing and scraping against the sheets and sleeping bag and what were from the outside. Even the beating of his heart had become confused and he didn't know if he was hearing that, or the sea, or something that was neither, the pulsing of the tiny life Laurel claimed to hold inside her.

"This is the life."

"What?"

"I told her that I swallow you twice a day."

"How uncouth."

"If we could just stay like this," Laurel said.

"There's people in India," Calvin said. "They spend their whole lives in this position. It's supposed to be very healthy."

"I think they do it sitting up."

"That would really be bad manners," Calvin said. "I've never done it sitting up." He tried to see himself as she did but couldn't. He was never able to imagine what he looked like. In the mirror he could see only his eyes, blue and hopeless, staring back at himself as if for an invisible camera. For a long time he had wanted his eyes to be pale and smudged, like paint dabbed carelessly on a canvas. But it was Laurel's eyes that he admired. In the mornings and the evenings when she was relaxed they were brown, but outside, touched by the sun, or anger, they slid everywhere from black to green: dark changeable eyes, like Johnny Tulip's, making his own seem that much less real, only further unnecessary proof of his whiteness, of his inability to survive here except by the good graces of those who surrounded him. But otherwise he could imagine himself: tall and bony, like his shadow flailing along the beach as he ran, tall and bony with straight dark hair and thick heavy arms.

Which now, pressed against Laurel's shoulders, seemed suddenly outsize, swollen beyond recognition by the continuous use of axe and chainsaw, the skin being gradually toughened by the weather but the inside still the same, weak and fluid, the nerves through his whole body still tied to Laurel's slightest motion, sparking now as she drew him in deeper, reviving the old tension in his stomach and chest, sending whispers of pain and electricity through his bones, circling his head in company with the suddenly louder noises of the birds and what seemed to be footsteps crunching through new snow and frozen leaves.

"It's just a fox or something," Laurel said. But it wasn't. The steps became clearer and closer. Stopped at the door, and then, without knocking or calling in, moved away again, the slow slightly blurred walk of Johnny Tulip, in the direction of the beach.

"Do you think he smelled us?"

"Of course," Laurel said. "Or looked in the window." And turning over his shoulder Calvin could see Laurel's leg, extended straight out from under the sleeping bag, up in the air where it would be visible from the door.

"I wish I wasn't jealous," Calvin said. "It seems so stupid."

"You might say that," Laurel said.

"Your breasts are like lemon drops," Calvin said.

Laurel pulled away and looked down. Calvin bent and licked his tongue along the place where there would have been a line, if she wore a bathing suit. The taste, like the smell, was faintly sweet and milky, not like lemon at all.

"You don't taste like lemon," Calvin said.

"Lemons have yellow bumpy skins."

He imagined that they had started to change already, the nipples spreading over the skin like a dark stain. When he licked them they were sweet too, the tiny hole in the centre a hot narrow line down the centre of his tongue.

"Pretty soon," Calvin said, "I guess I'll just fall into you."

"How romantic."

"I'm wildly in love with you," Calvin said. With his tongue he traced the tops of her eyebrows, stiff and salty. "Are you wildly in love with me?"

Her eyes filmed over and closed. "Really," Calvin said. "Maybe I *am* wildly in love with you." Small tears appeared in the corner of each eye. "Don't cry," Calvin said. He could feel his throat tightening again with anger and guilt.

Laurel opened her eyes again. The tears had dried already, small dried up ponds on the tops of her cheeks. "I'm sorry." She smiled unconvincingly. "Actually," she said, "I was going to go down to Vancouver today, with Johnny."

"What were you going to tell me?"

"Nothing," she said. "I could still go." Her hands on his back had formed small wet areas. She rubbed them around now, sliding her fingers in the valleys of his ribs, pushing his hair back from his face, twining her fingers into the hair at the back of his neck and pulling him to her, starting to move against him so he finally could distinguish himself from her, their bodies now so liquified he was sure the sheet must be soaked through to the mattress. In the night her face had been like a mask of desire, but now in the day it was flushed and human, needing him as he needed her, absolutely for this moment.

"Don't go," Calvin said.

"I didn't mean to bribe you," Laurel said. He felt like he was riding a wave so long and slow that he would never come but only explode in bits and pieces, his chest and stomach and back all held in some weird and perfect liquid rigidity. And Laurel too had stopped, was completely still except for a minute shuddering that locked him into her, would have held him there choked off forever if he had not suddenly panicked and pushed, his fear dissolving every-thing between them, taking Laurel too, whose eyes stayed open, staring into his, even when he could see that they had gone blank as he knew his own did seconds later, blocking out everything except a faint memory of the day by the stream and the sound of his own throat, caught, fighting for air.

Nine

Calvin found Johnny sitting on a log, staring out at the sea and whittling a small piece of cedar driftwood. There was no snow on the beach, only a fine layer of dampness that could have been from anything on a grey day like this. He sat down slowly beside him, his body still uncertain and liquid.

"Well," Johnny said. He turned to Calvin and grinned, his face wide and broken. He was clean-shaven today, and his hair had been slicked back and brushed.

"You look like you're about to apply for a job," Calvin said. "Or go to church." Then he remembered Laurel having told him that Johnny wasn't allowed to go to the church anymore because once, when he was drunk, he had exposed himself to the minister's wife. She had been so upset when her husband banned Johnny from the church that she went to apologize to him and asked him what she could do. He had told her he was ashamed. He said that he was going to the north shore of the island to meditate on his sins. Perhaps intrigued by the combination of the advertisement and the humility, she had gone with him. When she came back a month later, her husband, the minister, delivered a sermon on the meaning of charity.

Beside him, wedged into the sand, Johnny Tulip had a briefcase, a battered old brown leather briefcase with faint rubbed-off gold initials and a clasp assisted by a piece of string. Calvin wondered if this was Johnny's suitcase for accompanying Laurel to Vancouver.

"Come in and have some breakfast," Calvin said. "I'm starved."

"Okay," Johnny said. He stood up, and walked towards the water. "Look," Johnny said. He pointed to a round black object floating in the water. "A seal."

"It looks like a deadhead," Calvin said.

Johnny bent down and selected a round pebble. He threw it at his seal. He missed by about half the distance between him and it.

"That's terrible," Calvin said. He picked out a rock and threw it. It skipped on the water, veering off to one side when it hit.

"You see," Johnny said. "You called it a deadhead and now it doesn't like you. If you like a seal, it will always show you something."

"Do they ever sit up on the beach?"

"Sure," Johnny said. "All the time." He whistled, a curiously melodious whistle that seemed to contain several notes at once.

"I guess it didn't hear you," Calvin said.

Johnny whistled again, the notes so strangely spaced he seemed to be whistling in harmony. Calvin could see a big wave coming up on the deadhead. As the wave hit it, it rose up in the water, sleek and black, seemed to splash tiny fins, and disappeared.

In the cabin Johnny opened his briefcase. It contained not clothing but a map. He spread it out on the table. It was the government map of the island, with the logging roads drawn on in red. The map was in different colours, with light green to indicate the large areas of swamp and muskeg on the island. Calvin could see the lake where they had killed the deer, unnamed, and the river that wound down from it to the sea. The shape of the island was the shape of a short wide foot stamped into the sand.

Where the old logging camp was, near the old abandoned village, Johnny had marked a big X. And another big X right at the old village on the lake, Indian Lake, where his father had been buried beside the mortuary poles, wrapped in homespun linen so his body would disappear along with the already rotting poles. After Laurel had told him about this Calvin had started to pay more attention to the old tree trunks, moss-covered on the forest floor, noticing that they crumbled from the outside in. But when the wood on the outside was entirely dissipated and turned into rich humus with ferns and moss and strange wildflowers growing out of it, the centre of the log might still be perfectly sound, the red cedar splitting true and straight. In the end they were only shapes of logs that crumbled entirely when he jumped on them, the web-like structure collapsing into a scattering of fine red dust and moss, no hint being given of where the thousands of pounds of wood might have gone.

Looking at the map Calvin could see that the whole north end of the island, with the exception of the swampy areas which had only stunted and worthless trees, had already been logged. The lake he had gone to with Laurel had seemed to be surrounded by endless virgin forest; now he saw it was only the centre of a small island of unlogged territory, inaccessible because the ridges of high land which bordered it were themselves surrounded by land too wet to support roads.

The logging camp which had been in use for the last fifteen years was now uselessly in the midst of an exhausted area. He had driven through it once with Laurel and

Johnny, the expanses of scrub and slash marked by wooden signs saying TREE FARM, as if the sparse scattering of foot-high spruces growing through the vast heaps of abandoned logs and branches, which seemed themselves to constitute more wood than the trees on this land could have conceivably yielded, would someday grow into something other than a tangled waste of brush, rocks and eroded soil.

"They have to build the roads before the snow gets too deep," Johnny said, "so they can start cutting first thing in the spring." There was also a red X marked near the airport. "This is another place they're going to start," Johnny said. "They already logged there once. Now it's time to take off the second growth."

Calvin took a final look at the map and then went and sat on the couch, cup of coffee in his hand, absolutely at peace and contented, his legs too weak to support him and propped up on an old stump that was a combination coffee table, footstool and extra chair.

"They can have the south end of the island," Laurel said. "No one ever lived there anyway."

"Except Indians," Johnny Tulip said, startling Laurel who was standing at the counter, mixing pancake batter which tipped when Johnny Tulip spoke, but only half-spilled because Laurel recovered almost as quickly as she had slipped, her hand shooting out and righting the bowl.

"I didn't know that," Laurel said.

"Sure," Johnny Tulip said. "That was the best place to get logs for the cedar canoes." He had taken Calvin and Laurel once into the bush until they came to an almost perfectly circular clearing. In the centre of the clearing was a huge long log, roughly hewed into the shape of a canoe, its centre partly burnt out and its prow already split and rotting, seedlings taking root in the cracks.

"Everyone works in the camps," Calvin said, meaning not only the loggers who came from all over the coast and even the interior and south of the border, but the Indians too, who worked at the camps long enough to get the money to build a house or buy a fishing boat. Johnny Tulip was still leaning over the map, his elbow on the table and his body at a crazy angle, one leg crossed over the other.

"I don't work in the camps," Johnny said, in his lowest and most dignified voice.

"Artists don't have to work," Laurel·said. "They just drink and have a good time."

"That's right," Johnny said. "I'm waiting to be discovered."

"My father was an explorer," Laurel said. "If you would have stayed in one place, he would have found you."

Johnny was wearing one of his blue serge jackets. The back was creased and stained white from exposure to the salt spray. He opened up his jacket and withdrew a pen. "Here I am," Johnny said. He marked a red X in the centre of his forehead.

Laurel turned the radio on and, suddenly, loud and clear, a violin concerto came blasting into the cabin, the crashing introductory chords of the orchestra sounding as if they must have been produced by an assembly of the continent's high school orchestras. "Jesus," Johnny exclaimed, walking away from the radio and standing in the furthest corner.

"Sorry," Laurel said, turning it down. When the violin came on it was barely audible and she turned it up again.

"I always wanted to play the violin," Johnny Tulip said. "I would have been discovered if I'd played the violin."

"Or right field," Calvin said. "I always wanted to play right field." The stove had been fired up so hot to cook that the heat in the cabin was becoming uncomfortable. Calvin stood up and went over to open the door. At night it had been only a rectangular shadow but in the day it was grey and weathered cedar planks, pocked by scars of hooks and knives. He pushed the door open. The snow had all melted. The clouds were breaking up and he could see shafts of sunlight extending down through the trees on the way to the well, a tiny oasis of light that was swiftly moving towards him, and had, by the time he sat down again, come to rest on the sill of the door, transforming the day into instant summer as if the cold and rainy fall had never happened. A small black squirrel ran into the doorway, paused, cocked its head quizzically at the music, which seemed to be trying to work its way up to one of its frequent and sloppy crescendoes, and then ran away.

Laurel set the plates on the counter. The music from the radio stopped abruptly, was replaced by static which gradually dissolved into the voices of two airplane pilots.

"Going home tonight?"

"Can't wait to get laid?"

"What?"

"Can't you wait to get laid?"

"Wait for what?"

"I can't hear you."

"My fuel gauge isn't working."

"She'll never notice. They've done ten vasectomies here in the last two months."

"Look at that."

"Can't see it from here."

"Okay, see you later."

Instinctively Calvin looked out the window, trying to find the planes. PLANE DIES OF BROKEN FUEL GAUGE, the headline would read. But the pilot would escape of course, refusing to surrender for decades. The aftermath of the sex was like a blanket thrown over his nervous system. He felt calm and complacent. His hunger too was satisfied, so he ate slowly and pickily, trying to carve his pancakes into little islands, floating them in the syrup he had splashed on his plate, arranging them in a circle around its inside edge.

Johnny Tulip had finished his pancakes already, had gone to the stove to start another. "That goddamn logging company makes me sick," he said. "They get worse every year."

"Well," Laurel said. "They wouldn't get better." She swallowed. "I don't know why someone hasn't burned down that hotel."

Johnny turned to look at them from the stove and Calvin could imagine him doing it; it would be nothing at all.

"Too much insurance," Johnny said. "And besides, there wouldn't be anywhere to drink."

"You could get Mary Gail to poison his coffee," Calvin said, regretting it right away. Johnny just kept his back to them, flipped his pancake high in the air, and then, flipped it again, so high it touched the ceiling and came down all twisted, landing in the pan in a heap. Then he started to say something but it was lost in the burst of static as the radio went back to the music, the violin playing a solo now, weak and distant, the interference and the morning sun making it sound flat and out of place, insufficient.

The couch in the cabin was one of those huge padded monstrosities that were sold by department stores after the second world war, with thick backs and arms rimmed with machine-carved wooden trim. Resting on the trim, beside his plate, was the orange stone he had watched last night. Then it seemed alive and full of messages. Now it simply was cold and inert in his hand, as if it needed to be held and believed in if it was to convey anything. He put it in his pocket, wondering if carrying it would change it, conscious of it sitting like a cold growth against his thigh.

Laurel sat next to him, legs twisted under her, feet

pressed against his for warmth. Only Johnny was at the table, his plate on the map, hungrier than both of them put together, eating pancakes as fast as he could make them, filling the intervals between with slices of bread and jam. Although he was clean-shaven and his hair was brushed he looked exhausted and drawn, the lines under his eyes gathering into small dark pouches, his hands shaky and nervous as he worked at the stove, one time burning himself on the wrist, a hissing sound as all the water in the flesh evaporated, like spit on the red-hot iron, leaving a short red welt he carefully buttered and bandaged.

"Mary Gail," Johnny Tulip said, obviously disgusted, reminding Calvin for some reason of the way her arm had brushed him in the bar that first night. Then he saw Johnny exchange looks with Laurel as if there was something about Mary Gail, some secret aside from the fact that she lived with C.W. in the hotel which damned her absolutely and beyond mention.

"Well," Laurel said.

"Fucking whore," Johnny Tulip said. He was still standing at the stove and banged the skillet on the stove top for emphasis. Then reached into his jacket for papers and makings, rolling, Calvin noticed, his first cigarette of the morning, though usually he chain-smoked the whole day and evening. "I shouldn't say that about my own sister," Johnny Tulip said. His hands were shaking even worse now, and he was having trouble holding the flame to the end of the cigarette. The radio had run out of sound again, was just a low hum of electrical noise. Johnny turned it off and then went and closed the door. The sky had clouded over and a slight wind had begun to rise. On the beach the wind would be harsher, maybe even difficult to walk against. The thought of being trapped here for a day with Johnny Tulip and Laurel made Calvin feel edgy and he started trying to talk himself into going up the coast to look for rocks. Or even driving into town to get groceries and a newspaper. He realized he hadn't wanted to see one since he had come to the island, hadn't read anything except Laurel's occasional crossword puzzle and a few magazines in that whole time.

Laurel had dug her feet in deeper, but, despite that, he could sense she was moving away. He put his hand on her leg, pushing up her jeans, her ankle so small he could wrap his hand right around it. And cold too, icy. Her feet and legs were always cold. Sometimes it seemed that although she was perfectly balanced, with her cat-like reactions and speed, her ability to ingest endless quantities of alcohol and dope without being slowed down or made sick by them, she was actually fragile and delicate, barely able to sustain the circulation in her own body, her energy always gathered and waiting for some imaginary crisis.

Still grumbling and mumbling to himself Johnny Tulip sat down at the table with his new pancake, smoking too, covered it with butter and corn syrup.

"Well," Laurel said. "I don't know why you're so upset about Mary Gail now. You should have done something before she went to work at the hotel."

"Fuck," the cigarette bobbed in Johnny's mouth.

"I thought she needed a job, not a sermon."

"Anyway," Laurel said. "It's warm and it doesn't leak."

"Jesus," Johnny said. Somehow he had knocked his briefcase off the table. It landed upside down. When he picked it up a razor and a tube of toothpaste were left beneath it. He put them back in his briefcase. "A person has to stay clean," he mumbled.

Calvin went over to the stove and started assembling the percolator to make more coffee. Soon, from his briefcase or his jacket or, for all he knew, from some hidden place under the cabin, Johnny would produce a bottle of wine. The thought of wine just tired Calvin in advance. He still felt quiescent from the night and the morning, but instead of it being relaxed and good, it was only being drained, without the energy to make this into anything but the inevitable succession of mutually exhausting hours.

As he set up the percolator, prepared, on the stove, there was a knock on the door and it swung open. It was C.W.'s new mechanic, a boy from the mainland. His hair was wet, plastered down against his skull, and the legs of his pants were soaked.

"Come in," Calvin said. He closed the door behind the boy. The boy was short, as short as Johnny Tulip. His face was brown and smooth. If it weren't for his moustache it might have seemed he didn't need to shave.

"Take your coat off," Calvin said. "Sit down." The boy unzipped his coat, a dark green swamp coat with a hood that obviously hadn't worked. But his shirt looked dry.

"I'm sorry," the boy said. He was looking at Johnny Tulip.

"That's all right," Laurel stood up. "Do you want something to eat? You look frozen."

"It's your sister," the boy said, still looking at Johnny Tulip. "She and Mr. Smith had a fight and now she's in the clinic."

Johnny was on his feet right away, stuffing the map into his briefcase.

"She's okay," the boy said. "And she knocked out two of Mr. Smith's teeth."

"We'll have coffee first," Laurel said. "Then we'll all go." She was looking at the boy intently, her hand over her belly. "You might as well sit down," she said. "It might take a few minutes." The boy took off his coat and hung it on a hook beside the door. He was wearing a checked flannel shirt that had been washed so many times the colours had faded and run into each other. His back seemed almost outsize. The seams had parted on the shoulders and arms, showing ladders of thread. He walked over to the stump Calvin had been using as a stool, took it to the side of the room, and sat down. After the hotel, this cabin seemed explosive with colour and loose ends. He stood up again briefly, helping himself to some of Johnny's tobacco and a paper. He rolled the cigarette quickly, his nails, square and clean, digging neatly into the clean white paper, holding it still while he brought the edge up to his tongue. He saw them watching him and felt suddenly self-conscious.

The clinic was located in what used to be the hotel before C.W. Smith had built the new one, a long two-storey frame building that had been erected when the town was first put together by the logging company. At that time, almost fifty years ago, there had been more Indians and fewer whites, and the missionary and his wife had also been the doctor and the nurse, burying faster than they could convert. The succession of loggers, wars, and now tourists, had changed the balance, and gradually the necessity for some kind of hospital became obvious until finally they put one up. It survived thirty years and, it seemed, almost as many doctors, until it was destroyed in a mysterious fire.

When it burned they didn't even consider rebuilding it, no one offered to pay, and instead converted some of the unused space in the then run-down hotel into a kind of emergency ward. When C.W. built the new hotel, the clinic in the old one had been expanded, and even renovated—courtesy of an insecure provincial government and the logging company.

The boy had come to get them in the hearse. They walked back along the beach, and by the time they got to the road they were all soaked, Johnny Tulip's serge jacket stained black by the rain, bulging with the briefcase that he was trying to protect. He sat in the front with the boy, smoking incessantly, but not talking, his face seeming even bigger than usual because it was absolutely still, his big broken hands twisting in and out of each other. Once he turned to listen to something Laurel was saying and for a second Calvin saw him as he must have been thirty years before, his face smooth, handsome, and impersonal.

The boy drove fast, almost recklessly, to the clinic, accelerating on the corners and letting the wheels drift on the wet pavement, going eighty and ninety where the road was straight. Bumps that banged their heads into the roof of the truck seemed to disappear in the hearse's new and smooth suspension. When they got to the town and the gravel streets the boy slowed down. He glided carefully through the old section where the Indians lived overlooking the cove, past Johnny Tulip's mother's house which was ramshackle and weatherbeaten, a falling-down front, porched packed with old broken furniture, even a refrigerator.

The house showed no signs that anything unusual had happened and when they got to the clinic it looked ordinary too. When they met the doctor in the hall Calvin was startled to see how uncomfortable he was outside of the bar. He looked more like an outdoorsman than a doctor, his hands rough and red, protruding from the too-short sleeves of his white coat. His face was red too, flushed, and in a way that seemed more a combination of embarrassment and alcohol than of sun.

"In here," he said, extending his arm and motioning them into a room which seemed huge, bigger by far than their cabin, as if it had once been a ward intended for several patients. But now there was only one bed in it, a narrow iron hospital bed that seemed lost in this large space, despite the profusion of night-tables and flowers that surrounded it.

Mary Gail, her hair newly done and glowing, wearing what seemed to be several layers of negligees and bed jackets, was sitting up in bed, her back supported by two fat white pillows. Beside her, on a chair drawn right up to the bed, holding her hand contritely, was C.W. Although she was in the bed, Mary Gail looked by far the healthier of the two. In fact, Calvin thought, he had never seen her quite like this. It was as if she had spent the morning making herself resemble the women in some of the innumerable old magazines that haunted the island. Her lips were red and bow-shaped; she had outlined her eyes in black pencil, then added blue to her eyelids.

"You look fantastic," Calvin said.

Mary Gail smiled. "Thank you," she said.

C.W. definitely seemed to have lost. One eye was bruised black, just beginning to tinge yellow around the edges. His lower lip was split and swollen. There was a long scratch that extended from cheekbone to chin, like a messy red canal.

While everyone else found chairs and sat down, Johnny Tulip paced about the room. He put down his briefcase and drew out a knife, the same bone-handled knife he had had on the night of his birthday. He stood beside the windowsill and scraped at the peeling paint until some of it came away to reveal the red wood below. "Cedar," Johnny announced triumphantly. He scraped some more with his knife. The paint came off easily, barely clinging to the surface, the bonds broken by too many damp and unheated winters.

About to speak again, he suddenly noticed, on Mary Gail's night-table, half-camouflaged by a vase of yellow roses, a small bottle of brandy. And, beside it, decorated with roses to match those in the vase, was a box of chocolates. The brandy was unopened but the chocolates had been started; balled-up cellophane and brown paper cups littered the table. "Jesus Christ," Johnny said. He walked over to the bed and looked in the top of the box. He held the box in his hand and tipped it towards everyone so they could see that the top layer was almost gone.

"Jesus," Johnny Tulip said. He turned to Calvin. "What do you think?"

"I think I'll have butter pecan," Calvin said. The boy had slid his chair back towards the door. Johnny bent towards Calvin, holding the box closer. Calvin scanned the remaining chocolates carefully. "I don't see any," he said.

Johnny turned and held the box out to C.W. He held it just inches away from his face. C.W. stood up.

"Don't," Mary Gail whispered.

"I was just going to go for a piss," C.W. said. He spoke in his most formal midwest drawl, bowed his head in Mary Gail's and Laurel's directions, then left the room. The boy followed him.

"I think I'll go for a piss," Johnny said, mincing his words.

"Don't start a fight."

"Who's starting anything?"

"Then put your knife away," Mary Gail said. "God, you act like you're ten years old."

Laurel walked over to the window, pulled the knife out of the sill where Johnny had stuck it, and put it back in his briefcase.

"I don't know why I carry it," Johnny said. "I used to have one with a bottle opener and a pair of scissors."

"At least you don't need an opener for this," Mary Gail said, picking up the bottle of brandy, slitting the paper seal with her thumbnail, and then unscrewing the cap. She handed the bottle to Johnny.

"Go ahead," Johnny said. "You earned it."

"I can't. I have a bruised liver."

"What?"

"The doctor said I had a bruised liver." She looked at Johnny, batted her eyes, and tipped back the bottle. Johnny took a turn and passed it to Laurel. By the time Calvin got it, it was half empty. It was only a small bottle. The next time it came around there was just a small corner in the bottom.

"Here," Mary Gail said. She reached out and took it from him, her fingers soft and warm as they brushed his. She opened the door of her night-table and put the bottle in the bedpan.

"Can you go to the bathroom?" Johnny asked.

"Sure," Mary Gail said. "I just got a bruised liver."

There was a cough from the doorway. The doctor stood there. He was still wearing his white coat. "Excuse me," he said and walked into the room. He produced a thermometer from his pocket and stuck it into Mary Gail's mouth. "The wife's away," he said to no one in particular. While he waited for the thermometer he twined his fingers together and cracked his knuckles. He seemed exceedingly uncomfortable. He hadn't shaven that day and though the hair on his head was reddish brown, the beard that showed was completely white.

"Bruised liver is only my preliminary diagnosis," the doctor said. While he spoke he looked out the window. His voice seemed excessively loud. "As you know," he said, "the liver is located in the thoracic cavity." He poked himself in the chest. "Everyone has a liver," he said, "whether they are a man or a woman. Plants do not have livers."

He poked himself in the chest again and coughed. Then he found a cigarette in one of his pockets and lit it. As he blew out the smoke he coughed again, very lightly, the cough of an infant. "Excuse me," he said. "Doctors are not supposed to smoke." He smiled, and stepped back.

"The liver, he said, "is one of the most important organs. No man, or woman, can survive without a liver."

Calvin looked over to Laurel. "His wife left him," she mouthed.

"Liver pills won't help," the doctor said gloomily. "People think they will but they won't. Of course," he added, "I'm not an expert on livers. If you really want to know I'd have to take it out and do an autopsy."

Mary Gail giggled.

"I wouldn't recommend that in this case," the doctor said, speaking even more loudly, almost shouting. "It's a serious operation and we're short of staff at the moment."

"I could do it," Johnny said. "I always knew I could operate if I had do. I took out an appendix once."

"It was a dead mouse," Mary Gail said.

The doctor coughed again, a delicate and improbable cough. "The liver is a serious matter," he said. "I knew someone once who had worms in their liver."

"I wouldn't want to have worms in my liver," Mary Gail said. "What happened?"

The doctor cracked his knuckles. "I'm afraid it was terminal," he said in his loud voice. "Anyway," he said, "you shouldn't worry. Serious liver patients are always very sad."

"Well," Johnny said, "I guess she'll be okay then."

"Oh yes," the doctor said. "She's in good flesh. I don't expect any problems." He was looking intently out the window. The window faced not the street but the back of the clinic. Calvin stood up to see what the doctor was staring at. Outside the clinic, interwoven with small shrubs and trees, was a cemetery. Some of the graves had bright flowers on them, flowers so unseasonally colourful and healthy they were obviously plastic.

"I didn't know there was a cemetery here," Calvin said.

"It's full," the doctor said. "They sold the last grave in the spring." He looked wildly around the room for an ashtray, then stubbed his cigarette out on the windowsill. He cracked his knuckles. "I don't know where she could be," he said distractedly. "She's never done this before."

"How long have you been married?" Calvin asked.

"Oh," the doctor said. His voice level had dropped to

almost a whisper. "I don't even remember." He pulled out his pocketbook and started looking through it. It fell onto the floor, keys and change spilling out.

"I'll get them," Laurel offered, and was down on her knees, picking them up.

Johnny still seemed tense. He leaned towards Mary Gail. "Cheap bastard," he said, "only getting you a small bottle."

"I'm not supposed to drink anyway," Mary Gail said. She pointed at her stomach. "My liver."

"My ass," Johnny Tulip said. "What happened?"

Mary Gail looked out over the end of the bed. With her eyes made up and her pink jacket she looked like a beautiful stationary doll.

"Come on," Johnny said. He grabbed her wrist.

"I don't remember."

"Tell me."

Mary Gail tried to twist her arm away from Johnny. "Let go," she said.

"What happened?"

"I don't remember," she said. "I was drunk. He says I tried to shoot him." She jerked her arm away from Johnny and pulled the blanket up over her hands.

"You're not supposed to shoot people," Johnny said paternally.

"Thanks for telling me."

"Well," Johnny said. "I was only trying to help you."

Mary Gail laughed. Laurel and the doctor were trying to get everything back into his wallet. C.W. came back into the room. He had straightened his tie and buttoned up his vest. He took his coat from the back of his chair and put it on.

He leaned over Johnny and put his hand on Mary Gail's shoulder. "I'll see you later," he said.

"No," Johnny Tulip said, standing up abruptly,

knocking C.W.'s arm away from Mary Gail and driving his fist into C.W.'s stomach. C.W. was pushed back. But he straightened up easily and didn't seem to be hurt.

Calvin didn't know which way to move. He looked over to Laurel but she had her back to the whole room, seemed to be inspecting the cemetery.

"I want to see him," Mary Gail said.

"Okay," Johnny said. He shrugged and grinned strangely, as if he was trying to apologize. "I'm sorry," he said to C.W. "I guess I got carried away."

"That's okay," C.W. said. He seemed enormously tall. Johnny barely came up to his shoulder. C.W. flexed and adjusted his coat. He winked at Johnny. "It's a good thing you hit me on my mother's Bible," he said, "or you would have killed me." This time Johnny's punch doubled him right over, his head snapping down to meet Johnny's up-raised knee, its momentum temporarily interrupted, and then accelerated again by Johnny's other hand which came down out of the air like a wide-winged bird, chopping into C.W.'s neck so hard they both grunted at once. Which was the only sound there was until C.W., slowly assembling himself on the floor, his lip cut again and bleeding freely, spat some blood out.

Then he took out a handkerchief from his suit pocket, wiped his mouth and chin carefully, and stood up. There was no blood on his shirt or his suit. He looked down at Johnny Tulip. "You're still working for me," he said, turned and walked out of the room.

Ten

Johnny Tulip coughed. Hammered his hand into his chest and took a deep breath. C.W.'s feet shuffling slowly down the polished cedar floor of the clinic's hall, shuffling slow and stiff, like a proud old tight-assed bear. Mary Gail looking after him, her eyes ready to swell up and cry. Swell up and cry, swell up and die. Eyes tinged with blue, white blood that turns eyes blue. His mother's eyes had been blue too, white eyes, dead eyes. Huge soft blue eyes, soft like sponges, that the doctors took out: first one when her sight was so bad that she couldn't even see the wall, and then the other, when they said she would die if they left it in. And each time he had travelled down to Vancouver with her, on the boat. First he believed they could do something for her and he was happy the whole time, staying in the house of the missionary's brother, playing his fancy grand piano between visits to the hospital. But the second time was worse. He only wanted them all to be wrong, for the boat to be obliterated by the sea, which refused to co-operate, laid flat and dead the whole way, both ways. Bringing him back like a fool and a traitor, leading his own mother, blind, with bandages swathed around her head and a whole suitcase full of pills and ointments. "You'll be the doctor now," they had told him. But he wasn't. Only sick, his body torn and emptied by some city fever that left him in bed for a month.

The heel of his hand was sore and his leg didn't want to stand straight. C.W.'s jaw had hurt like iron, smashing into his knee, teeth sharp as axes. He reached into his pocket for tobacco and papers, pinching the tobacco between his fingers to draw it out of the package, laying it in the paper automatically, his thumbs bending automatically too, the whole thing so fast now, he hardly felt the paper against his fingers, or tasted the glue that lay in a thin yellow stripe at the edge of each paper, that he used to hate so much he would spit on his finger and rub it against the paper. Lit a match and drew the smoke in, smoke dry and grey, soaking into the coatings of fluid and tar that seemed to line his insides, screening out everything, an armour only liquor, salt, and smoke could cut through.

"You bastard," Mary Gail said.

"I'm sorry." The urge to cough was always there, as if some part of him was still convinced he could tear whatever it was out of his insides, bring it up and leave it somewhere.

"It doesn't matter," Laurel said. Liquor, salt and smoke and Laurel too, more than anything else, everything she said or did living right inside of him, even her voice so familiar and so close it seemed to come from himself, her words echoes of something he had just dreamed.

And then her too, going down the hall, her steps quick and light, Calvin's hesitant, as if he was following behind her. And from the window he could see them come out into the cemetery, the strange white man's cemetery where all the bodies got eaten while the stones stood above them, to last forever. Laurel's arm was around Calvin's waist, close, like a vine, holding onto him or holding him up, it was impossible to tell.

"He's not that bad," Mary Gail said.

"She needs him."

"He's just strange here," Mary Gail said.

"Strange," Johnny Tulip said. And sat down on the bed beside his sister. Looked closer at her eyes, brown eyes with big wedges of blue and yellow, their colours broken and smashed by blood and maybe C.W. too, who had taken the rifle from her and thrown her across the room.

In one hand he held the cigarette. The other he put on the blanket and she picked it up, surrounded it with her own, hot and steaming, like always, her skin so warm it seemed her whole chest must be filled up with her heart, squirting blood out so hot and fast.

"Well," he said. "You don't look too sick."

"I feel okay."

"My preliminary diagnosis," Johnny said, trying to stretch his face so it would be longer and narrower, holding his mouth in tight and small.

"Liver," Mary Gail said. "I never even thought about my liver."

"It's where you keep your shit," Johnny said. Mary Gail squeezed his hand. Dumb women with their men. Sometimes seeing Laurel with Calvin made him feel amost sick; but Mary Gail with C.W. was worse, made him feel nothing at all, only more death on the island, stones and cement that would survive the bodies.

"You shouldn't have done that."

"The bastard tried to bite me," Johnny said. He pulled up his trouser leg, old blue trousers that had belonged to Harry Jones and were so wide they were wearing out rubbing against each other. On his knee a ring of red marks was indented in his skin. "See?" Johnny said. "He's a killer." He laughed.

"Johnny."

He stood up, and crossed the room to the window.

"You can't stay."

"Fuck." Laurel and Calvin were still standing in the

cemetery, holding hands, completely involved in each other.

"Well," Mary Gail said. "It's not going to be the same."

"Move home."

"No," she said. "If I leave, he'll do something to you."

Johnny coughed. It was starting to rain, slow big drops splattering against the glass. Laurel and Calvin looked up at the sky, pulled their jackets tighter around them and started walking away from the unprotected graves, towards a grove of trees that lay in back of the cemetery. His knee still hurt. And his hand too, felt like it must be broken. So old now his body was scarred by everything it touched.

"He won't do anything," Johnny said. He laughed carefully, trying not to antagonize the new pressures he could feel building up, as if the creature inside him was going to get whatever revenge C.W. couldn't.

"I can't leave now," Mary Gail said.

"Okay. Who cares?" He stretched his hands out in front of him, wriggled his fingers experimentally.

"You going to keep playing there?"

"Oh no," Johnny said. "I'll just run and hide under my father's grave until he shoots you. Then I can cry at your funeral." He never seemed to grow used to the way his own voice rasped, bubbling through the liquid that kept growing in him, like raw eggs, yolks like pupils smashed apart in his throat and chest.

"Don't keep going there," Mary Gail said.

"I need the money." The rain was coming harder and faster, streaming off the window in sheets. Soon it would get colder too, the days brief and the sun making its short daily run way over in a corner of the sky. The wind stripped of its heat by the sea so the rain would drive right through to the bones. It would be better if it snowed this winter. Snow was lucky, Harry Jones used to say, when he had the trap line that cut through the forest. Harry Jones, dead too, squeezed out of shape by a tree. There were still some Indians trapping on the island, but not many. It was easier to work for the logging company or fish.

There had been snow on the ground in the morning, drifted across the road in a thin film, buried quickly in the long grass of the ditches. Snow never froze your bones as it fell. Or soaked you through so the wind could take away your warmth.

Johnny pushed his shoulders back, tried to make some space in his chest. It was still early, afternoon. But he felt tired and sore, his knee aching where it had met C.W.'s teeth, his hand sharp and painful. In the morning it had snowed but there had been no sign on the beach. He had sat on a log, trying to guess the coming winter, but hadn't been able to tell anything at all. Only the sea had been present, breathing so slow and so patient into the sand, waiting to fill its endless belly again.

Mary Gail stretched and pulled the covers up to her neck. "I feel so sleepy," she said. "I don't know what's wrong with me." She had always passed from waking to sleeping with extraordinary speed, her voice dropping off and her eyes falling shut. And now it was the same. As soon as she announced it, she curled up under the cover, wrapped her arms around the pillow, and closed her eyes. She seemed aware that he was about to leave. "See you soon," she mumbled, her voice thick, and then flopped about, her back to Johnny and the door, air already humming through her half-open mouth.

Her face still seemed adolescent to him, barely formed, the skin bumpy and imperfect from chocolate bars and soft drinks, her bones just reaching their defined state, unsure whether they would have that vague sharpness and fragility that her mother's did, or like his own, become round and blunted.

Mary Gail was born after their mother had already

become thick and fat, too old to have children. She only had one eye left then; she held Mary Gail up to the light but couldn't see her at all, only felt her with her hands, kneading and shaping her as if she had only succeeded in giving birth to so much raw matter that still needed to be formed. Mary Gail, the youngest by far, twelve years younger than the next, Victoria, named after the old Queen of England the missionaries always talked about. Fat Queen Victoria with her skinny husband who live somewhere in a cold wet stone house, like a grave. Fat Victoria who painted her face and lived in picture frames in the parlours of the missionary's houses. Posed above the piano and so proper that all the Indian women fell in love with her, going to the missionary's house for tea, all naming their children for her.

When Harry Jones came back from the Panama Canal he had spent a year making a rowing boat, a strange-shaped scow that looked like a hollowed-out gourd and moved only slowly and with difficulty. But it was steady and wouldn't sink. He named it Victoria too; after his daughter Victoria who was barely born then, barely old enough to be taken out in it. Her face then round and placid, Johnny would hold her, kicking to be held up to the wind and wanting the water to be blown at her.

Mary Gail settled deeper into her bed, pushed the blankets off her shoulders, starting to heat up, as always. By the time she woke she would be covered by only the sheet. When she was a baby it was Victoria who had taken care of her, taken care of her and her mother too, rushing about the house like a demon, giving orders to everyone.

The rain had slowed down. Johnny Tulip stood by the window, gave in finally to the cough that had been building up in his chest, coughed once, hit his chest with the flat of his hand, and coughed again, feeling the liquid peeling away from his lungs, cleaning a small patch. He took a piece of kleenex from Mary Gail's night-table and spat into it, rolled it up quickly without looking. Soon the whole island would be cycled through his lungs, returned to itself mixed with blood and kleenex. His hands, he noticed, were shaking. The morning he found Victoria on the beach his whole body had started shaking, his teeth chattering and bones knocking together as if he was going to fall apart. Forty-one years old then, the day of his birthday, so drunk and so sad he had left his brother and gone to sit on the beach with one last bottle of wine, wait for the sun to come up.

Walking on the beach that morning, half a moon, and the sense of someone else's presence. That was the summer Laurel Hobson had first come up from the city, young and timid, like a rabbit, an aura fluttering nervously in and about her.

His hands were still shaking. Johnny Tulip reached into his coat again, for the tobacco and papers. The pants he was wearing were Harry Jones's but the coat had belonged to a missionary. The tobacco now was in his palm. He worked it automatically, watching the small hooked pieces seal together with the oils of his skin, roll up into a small cylinder which he inserted into the paper, laid it in soft and floppy, like a tired fish, like he had been with Laurel the first time; but not the second.

When he was young the lines in his palm had hardly been visible, impossible to read or trace. Now they were cut in deep, doubled and tripled by small lines that ran alongside, echoing and criss-crossing the main ones. The cigarette looked lost and artificial in his hand. And now, when he played the piano, his hands seemed too big and stiff to do anything. Only memory made it possible, memory and the separate life of his bones which still jumped to the music effortlessly, no matter how drunk or sad, jumped and moved across the keys so quick and easy it sounded exactly like one of those pianos with the handle and the punched paper tapes.

In sleep Mary Gail's face was adolescent, almost babyish. The summer Laurel had come Mary Gail had been only fifteen; and so slow developing she might have been ten, her body a pile of sticks thrown together, skinny and snake-like, ribs jutting out, curved bones grabbing round her belly.

Six years ago Victoria had died and the world had stopped and begun again—divided in half: walking on the beach, half a moon in the sky that was starting to lighten and turn purple with the morning. Half a moon and half a sky too, one side opened and stretching out forever across the sea, the other closed off by the cliffs and trees. It was the same stretch of beach where he had first met Laurel Hobson and her friend, huddled into the rain, unable to keep a fire. Laurel who had been useless and white, crouched by the smoking wood, supple and young, looking up at him out of the smoke and he had seen it right away. And when he brought them home the others recognized her too: sitting beside Victoria in the kitchen they looked almost like twins, each the shadow of the other.

Laurel looked like Victoria's ghost, a white omen so innocent and unaware that Victoria had to leave the house, stay somewhere else for the whole week Laurel was there. She moved back only when she heard how Laurel had fallen and gone back to the city on a stretcher.

Walking on the beach, the stones and logs gradually jolting his body loose from the wine, the morning light and the slow sounds of the sea moving through him. When Laurel was being put onto the plane on the stretcher he had almost wanted to go with her, watch over her at the hospital and bring her back. Not sure if he had claimed her that morning on the porch or if something terrible had happened. The whole summer passed watching Victoria get sicker, always being reminded by her of Laurel, her quickness, the strange divided way she had taken him inside her, trying to fool him and herself too. And him drunk that first night, soft and floppy, the old fish who wasn't going to make it.

"Johnny." He went over to the bed and sat beside Mary Gail. After mumbling his name, she seemed to have gone back to sleep. He lit his cigarette, the stray bits of tobacco at the end flaring quickly, threw the match on the floor. Looked down at Mary Gail and saw that her eyes were open. "Johnny. I don't know what's going to happen." She curled into him, took his arm in her hands, pressed her face against it.

"Who knows?" Johnny said. He laughed and coughed. "Everything will be the same."

Six years ago everything had divided in half. His brother had given him the bone-handled knife and slashed it through the air, cutting the world into two parts. Like a woman. Like the half moon lighting half a sky. Six years ago he would not have let C.W. walk out of the room, would not have shut himself off from Mary Gail. Six years ago he had been so innocent and drunk, walking up the beach on the morning of his own birthday, his head filled with thoughts of that quick, sly white girl who had stolen something from him.

Later his mother had told him that she had seen it all: Laurel flying to the island again, her back stiff but mended, Victoria knowing it too, the doctor's verdict and Laurel's return hanging over her like a feast.

With his new knife in his belt and the bottle of wine under his arm he had walked up the beach, oblivious to Victoria, who must have already been dead for hours, being dragged in by the tide.

"Johnny." Mary Gail looked up at him. And then closed her eyes was asleep again, her hands still wrapped tight about his arm.

Walking on the beach, Johnny Tulip had come to the cliff where Laurel had hurt herself. He had been so drunk, so full of his birthday wine and thoughts of her, he didn't notice that someone had already been there. Just sat down on his birthday bottom and slid carefully down her path.

In those days his stomach was seated more solidly in his body, resisted nothing. He wiped the pebbles and sand off his trousers and stood up at the bottom of Laurel's slide. Opened the last bottle of wine and rinsed out his mouth. Sour and red, the wine then, sour and thin, running into all the dry corners of his mouth, in between his teeth, trickling down his throat as slow as the sea.

Later he thought it must have been then, the moment when he slid down the cliff on his pants and his heels, coming up quickly with the bottle tucked beneath his arm, swinging out to be opened, that his sister Victoria had been brought into shore. He had used the knife to slit the paper seal. The handle was made of polished bone; the steel blade had come all the way from England, sharp and hard. His brother had made him a sheath for it too, a sheath of deerhide which he knotted to his belt with a thong. He spat the wine out quickly, thin and red, spat it through the cracks between his teeth. Too drunk to do it well, he could feel thin streams drying on his chin. Thin streams of red, like the tears of his mother, pink with the blood from her operations, gathering in the broken criss-crossed skin that surrounded her sockets like dark frozen sand.

With the first drink the clouds that had been lying on the horizon, patiently waiting for the sun to rise over their edge and burn them away, made instant revisions of their plans and began to rise and sweep across the sky. The wind came up with them, sudden and wet. In minutes it was raining, a cold fall rain that carried the warning of the winter with it.

He kept moving up the beach, closer to the trees for shelter from the wind. Even when he found the trail that edged into the forest, behind the first rows of trees, he didn't notice she had been there before. An old trail, broken and set first by deer, then trampled wider and muddier by those who walked up to the old cabin, an old abandoned cabin that had a roof, a wood stove, and a lock.

And it was only as he pushed the door open, saw Laurel's gear strewn on the floor of the cabin, red nylon pack with the airline baggage ticket wired to it, that he began to register the faint smell of smoke, the broken lock, the half-memory of a few shallow footprints in the sand, only partially washed away by the one intervening tide.

Laurel was awake as soon as he came in, twisting around and sitting up in her sleeping bag. He remembered turning back to close the door, close out the grey half-morning light that was now too soon. But even through the one old window he could see her well enough: grey and sallow from the months in the hospital, turning stiffly to meet him.

He remembered too that at first she didn't recognize him. But then, as he stepped closer, of course she did. "You scared me," she said. Her voice silver and formal, the words bouncing off each other like hard bits of glass.

He crouched down at the foot of her sleeping bag, keeping his distance. Her voice so removed and dead. She had been more real in his dreams than she was now.

She had already found a cigarette, was holding a lighter in front of it. Snapped it and sucked in the first smoke. Then she tossed the package to him, easy and unafraid. Victoria's ghost, already breathing in her death. He looked around the cabin and saw that Laurel had brought warm clothes and food, as if she intended to stay around for a while.

"Well," she said. "Maybe I scared you." She smiled. The expressions on her face were like unconvincing masks, like her words, distant and foreign. He could feel the wall he was putting up, pushing her back, keeping her away from wherever it was she had already crossed into him.

"Louise told me that you carried me to the road," Laurel said. "She said I better thank you." She smiled again.

"That's okay," Johnny said. The smoke from her cigarette was making him dizzy. His head swam with bits of dreams from the last three months, images and tastes of Laurel woven into every night's sleep. He was holding her cigarettes in his hand. The sharp corners of the package bit into his skin. The cabin was filled with the smell of her cigarette, with the smell of cold woodsmoke too. He went over to the stove and looked inside. The fire was long dead, the wood unburnt. He tapped the stovepipe. Soot rattled down.

"It gets all jammed up," Johnny Tulip said. "And there's nowhere for the smoke to go." He tapped the pipe again, kept hitting it until the noise stopped. There was some kindling piled near the door. A hatchet too; it was new and encased in shiny brown leather. He took out his new knife and peeled shavings off the kindling.

"I wasn't cold," Laurel said. "It's wasteful to burn wood when you're not cold."

"Okay," Johnny said. "I'm cold." When he put a match to the shavings they flared up instantly, filling the stove with flame and noise.

"I guess I'm not good at making fires," Laurel said.

Her skin was grey and colourless. Her eyes too, as if there had been nothing she wanted to see. Not like Victoria's which were black and without depth, so black

149

they seemed to have already known everything. No white blood in Victoria's eyes. No white blood in Victoria at all, except somewhere deep in her belly where it had all pooled together to eat her away, smashing apart her womb the way it had their mother's eyes, white and soft, white and dead.

Laurel put the cigarette to the floor, rolled it carefully so the ash came off the tip. The fine sudden angles of her fingers were so totally Victoria's movement that for once he could feel it in his own hands, what it would be like to have these narrow bone needles sewn through his flesh.

"At least you could offer me a drink," Laurel said. "You don't break into a young lady's room in the middle of the night unless you've got a present for her."

He passed her the bottle, watched her tip it back, pull it quickly away from her mouth when she tasted it. She inspected the label and handed it back.

"It was a present for me," he said. "My brother's so mean you wouldn't believe." Through the small window he could see the sun was beginning to lighten the clouds, push long yellow triangles up into the sky. He had shaved the previous morning, for his birthday. He pushed his hair back from his face and wiped his eyes.

She was wearing a blue cotton shirt, too big for her, the collar turned up and the sleeves pushed up to her elbows. She was trying to look self-sufficient and poised but she seemed lost and grey, like a discarded doll. Scattered about the floor and on the small counter beside the stove, were all the things she had brought with her from the mainland: the small hatchet, a knife, a few packages of dried food, a pile of clothes that seemed to be mostly a sweater and a nylon raincoat.

Johnny Tulip stood up and stretched. His brother had given him a bottle and a knife. One to drown the world. And the other to cut it in half, to mark his birthday with that hole between the two that already seemed to have swallowed the past, started the world over again with one brief gesture that had finally led him up the beach to this cabin with this strange girl who didn't know how to fuck or light a fire or even tip back his own last birthday wine without dribbling it down her chin and throat.

In his dream she had been different than this, shy and nervous like a doe. Now she seemed curiously placid and tired. He yawned. He didn't want to face this whole day without sleep.

"You can lie down here," Laurel said.

He stretched out and she put her arm around him. Her hand was cool on his forehead, cool and white, long fingers like wind on his scalp. She was still sitting up and his head was against her stomach. He could hear all the strange sounds it was making, bubbling soprano sounds, delicate sounds, the formal sounds of a foreign woman's stomach. He wondered what could have happened to Victoria's guts, whether she'd been attacked for fucking the wrong person or at the wrong time. He'd gone to talk to the doctor once but when he got to the doctor's house the doctor was out, fishing, his wife said. This meant he was standing in a rust-coloured stream somewhere, wearing rubber boots that came up to his shoulders and a red peaked cap, casting out his line with a cotton insect at the end.

Laurel's stomach was bubbling like a stream too, like a waterfall in the forest, like a bottle of beer being poured into a tall glass. He turned and poked at her shirt with his face, until he could feel her belly against his cheeks. One ear was pressed to her stomach. She held her hand over the other, her palm warm and cupped. With his hand he searched out her hip, slid under the nylon sleeping bag. Her legs moved apart for him as he slid down further. Then snapped together quickly, trapping his hand where she wanted it to be.

She held his head against her belly and he could hear

nothing of the wind or the rain or trees rubbing up against the cabin. Only the liquid choir of Laurel's plumbing, growing louder and higher. He moved his head down further, following his hand. In the end it was as it had been before: his trousers down around his ankles, his belt buckle digging between them. Only this time she was ready, sucked him in and held him fast, like a worm gripped by a robin.

He tried to work himself free. Her hips had gone hysterical. The noise of their parts sucking and bubbling against each other was louder than her stomach had ever been. He felt possessed, pumping like a madman trying to deliver this greedy white ghost. His back was scalded and aching. He could feel the sweat pouring out of him in torrents; he had never sweated like this—even the missionary's wife had yielded more quickly.

"Please," Laurel said.

He opened his eyes and saw the dead image of his sister Victoria. He screamed in sudden panic and fear. Laurel relaxed, her back arched and her legs stuck straight out. He swarmed inside her, broken into ten million eggs.

He stood outside in his birthday rain, pissing against the wall of this old cabin. His stomach was covered with dried sweat and juices. For this moment he looked as he had before his brother killed the past: square and muscular, brown, a thin dent around his waist where he tightened his belt. He dug his feet into the wet black earth, pushed so it came up between his toes, now knobby and calloused from decades of shoes.

When he went inside, Laurel was getting dressed, tucking her shirt into her jeans, heavy socks and moccasins on her feet. His own clothes were in a heap on the bottom of the bed: the missionary's jacket and Harry Jones's pants, a shirt that the missionary's wife had sewn for him, embroidered across the shoulders. Laurel had put more wood in the stove, was trying to raise some water to a boil. Outside he hadn't even noticed the sun, but here, from the window, he saw it struggling to cut through the clouds.

"It's going to be a nice day," Laurel said.

Johnny started putting on his clothes. The missionary's wife had made the shirt out of soft cotton, sewn it with careful tiny stitches so it would stay together for a long time. He felt as young as he had the first time he put it on. Something in his chest lodged momentarily. He coughed. He tightened his belt around his waist. They would drink the tea and then they would walk down the beach, to the village, to find out what had happened to Victoria.

It was raining worse than ever by the time they were ready to go outside. And they found Victoria long before they got to the village. Her body was washed in just on the other side of the cliffs. She was icy cold from her hours in the sea, swollen and bruised from the battering against the sand and rocks. He pulled her away from the water, hoisted her up over his shoulder. He felt as drowned as her, stiff and rubbery. His father dead had made him cry and come apart. Victoria dead made him numb. He didn't dare look at Laurel. He carried Victoria up the beach, laid her under the trees, covered her body with branches and rocks.

Eleven

C.W. leaned back in his chair, put his feet up on the desk. His office was a shambles. There were papers piled on the desk and on the floor. The closet door was open, clothes strewn throughout it, the rifles leaned sloppily against the back. At one time C.W. had kept a picture of his wife and her cats on his wall. Now it had been torn down, victim of one of his battles with Mary Gail. There was a patch of plaster showing through the paint where the hook had been.

The curtains were closed, as always. Recently he had installed bulletproof windows. The boy had helped him screw them into place. "No use taking any chances," C.W. had said. He had the windows flown in specially from Vancouver, ordering them two weeks ago, the day after Johnny Tulip jumped him in the clinic.

His lip had swollen up so badly it was painful to shave. Now C.W. sprouted a short growth of beard, the hairs spread evenly over his face, all the way down from his cheekbones. Some of them were black and others were grey. There seemed to be no real pattern to the colours so the effect was, with the clean shirts and striped suit he still wore, to make him look more eccentric than ever, a rich old prospector from a used up movie set.

"You got to know to handle a woman," C.W. said. He stretched and put his hands behind his head.

The boy nodded. It was still early in the morning and he felt sleepy. Over the bulletproof glass they had hung the old curtains, patterned cotton from a department store. The grey morning light barely succeeded in showing through the thin material.

"The first woman a man ever knows is his mother," C.W. said. "There's some that say if you can't get along with your mother you'll never get along with anyone."

The boy nodded again. It was not difficult to imagine C.W. in striped diapers and vest, being wheeled about Great Falls, Montana in a pram.

"Did you get along with your mother?"

The boy shrugged. The cuts on his hands had healed completely now. There were only small pink hieroglyphs on his skin to show where they had been. Soon they would be grown over too.

"No one ever wants to talk about philosophy," C.W. complained. He reached into his vest pocket and withdrew a small flat box. He had given up cigarettes after he stopped shaving, had switched to small cigars. He offered the box to the boy, who declined, and then stuck a cigar between his teeth. There was now a small rim of gold showing. The teeth hadn't been lost, only loosened.

"My father was a great one for talking," C.W. said. "He had a set of The World's Greatest Books and he used to go down to the basement after supper and read from them out loud. He often used to say that what made man different from the animals was his mind." C.W. tapped his temple reflectively.

"The human mind is a wonderful thing," C.W. said. "It

never rests." He puffed on his cigar. He looked carefully at the boy. "Of course there are exceptions," he admitted.

"Oh yes," the boy said.

"For example," C.W. said, pointing his cigar at the ceiling, "my mother was never much of one for thinking. No. Most women don't think. You have to know that."

The boy shrugged.

"You take Mary Gail," C.W. said. "Of course I don't have anything against Indians. You put a suit on an Indian and he might as well be white." Before they flew their first mission, the whole crew of their bomber had trained together. Then the navigator had been killed, almost by mistake it seemed, a stray piece of shrapnel that had ripped through the metal skin of the plane. The new navigator was an Indian. Somehow he had been to college. But he didn't talk too much. One afternoon C.W. told him about the dream he always had, the long line of soldiers falling crazily to the ground. The next day the Indian was gone, just disappeared from the base. He came back a week later, drunk. They had to put him in the hospital.

"The whole world is in Montana, is what my father taught me," C.W. said. "Have you ever been to Montana?"

"No," the boy said, "I haven't."

"It's the third largest state in the Union," C.W. said. "Not counting the new ones. I don't know anything about them."

"Is it dry or is it swamp?"

"What?"

"Montana."

"There's no swamps in Montana," C.W. said. "Montana is a state of mountains and plains."

"It sounds nice," the boy said.

"You have to see it." C.W. adjusted himself in the chair. "Of course the whole world is anywhere," he said. "Even in your little finger. Plato said that."

156

"Plato?"

"He was an ancient Greek philosopher," C.W. said. "He used to go out into the streets every day and speak his mind. My father liked to read his books out loud in the basement. He was a very important thinker."

"Oh."

C.W. composed his face in a solemn way that the boy had never seen before. "Every man is unique," C.W. said. "That is why we live in a democracy." He put his feet down and pulled himself towards the desk. He opened the top drawer and brought out some black horn-rimmed glasses. He put them on and scratched his incipient beard. On his desk were piled letters from lawyers, the logging company, the government.

The boy was sitting in an armchair facing the desk. He was holding his empty coffee cup, swirling the remains around in the bottom. When C.W. came up to his desk the boy leaned forward too, deposited his cup on the round plastic tray Mary Gail had brought in from the kitchen.

C.W.'s beard felt like blunt needles in his skin, each hair grown swollen and itching in its pore. Now he could hardly sleep in the same bed as Mary Gail. He woke up almost every hour, brought sharply awake with his heart pounding so hard it seemed it wanted to smash right out of his chest. But the dream was always gone, cut away as if with a razor. All he would remember were colours—red and black, flames and smoke like a forest fire or a child's dream of hell—and his own panic. Sometimes these censored dreams were prefaced by dreams he could remember: long, convoluted war-movie scenes. Men being marched up and down the halls of stone castles. Endless sets of steps. Long meaningless interrogations. The sharp European sun lighting up brick walls as he was carelessly pushed in front, blindfolded, the heat of the morning unbearable.

Beneath the papers C.W. had a big calendar. The

month was October and each day's square was filled with C.W.'s writing, a tiny almost illegible script. Beside it was one of the government maps of the island. C.W. had marked the camp where Johnny and Laurel had blown up the tractor. Around the camp were drawn concentric circles, stretching out to the main road on one side and a lake on the other. This lake was called Indian Lake, named by someone who had run out of names but known about the abandoned village on its shore.

Pencil lines for roads radiated out of the camp like spokes from a hub. One of the spokes, one that went towards the main road, was where Johnny Tulip's father had killed himself. Another went right to the abandoned village on Indian Lake, where he was buried.

Thinner lines connected the radiating spokes. The plan looked like a cobweb, like a unicycle dressed up for a parade. With his horn-rimmed glasses C.W. inspected the map, tapped a sharp pencil against its edges. The roads were all numbered and those numbers reappeared in the squares of his calendar.

"I'm just trying to get things done," C.W. said. "You'd think it was the end of the world just because we were going to cut down a few trees. No one ever looks at them anyway." He watched the boy. He might have been one of the enemy soldiers in the dream, smooth and foreign, moving as if he owned something secret.

The boy followed C.W.'s line of sight to the cupboard, where it rested contemplatively on the three rifles stacked there. "Well," the boy said, "I'd better get started." The back of the hearse was already packed with boxes of dynamite and fuses, waiting to be drawn down the highway, driven carefully over the rough logging trails to the hub of the wheel. Where it would spread out again, creating new roads through the trees and rock.

When he left the office the boy took the coffee cups and the tray back to the kitchen. There were no bulletproof windows here but it too seemed in a state of siege, unwashed dishes piled on the new aluminum counters, half-wrapped food left out, some of it going bad. Mary Gail was standing at the sink, soapsuds spilling out onto her and the floor, a stack of clean dishes slowly rising from the wreckage.

"I'm sorry," the boy said. "I should have done these. I didn't know you would be coming back today."

Mary Gail turned to answer him and he could see her eyes were puffy and red from crying.

"I have to go to the camp," the boy said. "I'll come back and help you later."

"I'll come for the ride," Mary Gail said. She rescued her arms from the water, shook them dry over the dishes, and followed him out to the car.

They found a place only a few miles out of town. She pointed to the side of the road and he slowed down, parked in a slight cusp. Then she led him up a slippery grass bank and into the forest. They came to a grove where the red cedars were particularly tall, formed a ring extending hundreds of feet into the air, pushing the sky up into a tiny and unrecognizable swirl of blue and grey.

"Please," the boy said.

There had been one time before, in the boy's room at the hotel. They hadn't heard C.W. until the noise of the handle being tried, the door against the frame as it either rattled or closed gently.

"I don't know."

The boy lay down in the thick needles, lay down on his back and looked up at the sky. He couldn't see much. The clouds were trying to cover the island in layer after layer of thin grey gauze. But today it wasn't enough, it was too windy, and they only succeeded in making the blue streaked and sporadic, a cold and sunless day. It was hard to believe that this same tiny sky stretched in a huge bowl over the prairies, grew thick and smoky over Toronto.

Mary Gail kneeled beside him. She unbuttoned his jacket and his shirt. The air surrounded him quickly, cold and damp. But where she touched it was warm and alive. Her lips and tongue were curiously slack, a hot water spider insanely skating in the rain.

"He's so old."

The boy pushed his stomach up in the air, breathing in the space between his belly and his spine.

"He's got hair on his chest and he has bad dreams all night."

"Everyone dreams," the boy said.

"I dream when I have something to dream," Mary Gail said. "But not every night. A person that dreams every night would go crazy."

There were hundreds of paths on his skin, vast networks connected to the air by the absence of her tongue.

"My mother never dreams," Mary Gail said. "But she's blind. She has the second sight."

The clouds came and went from the small sky he could see. But no matter what the colour of the sky, the air felt cold and rainy, wet air heavy with oxygen that blasted so strongly from the trees on this island that even when he went from the road to the forest there was a noticeable difference, a sharp.current through his blood that erased everything else.

The cedars rose up absolutely straight, hardly wider at the bottom than at the top. The only branches were near the crown. Further down all the green had died, starved for sun, leaving only small brown stubs protruding blunt and tooth-like from the trunk.

When they stood up their bodies looked soft and bumpy beside the trees. And their skins, mottled and divided into zones by clothes and the sun, were plastered with needles, like door-prizes. Driving in the hearse again it was her feet that he noticed, bare feet dug into the thick carpet, short and square, the toes curiously arched and of almost equal length.

Mary Gail sat close to him, her hand moving nervously from the seat to his thigh. She turned the radio on, adjusted it impatiently. "Sometimes we get the station from the mainland," she said. But this time there was nothing, not even static. She shook her head. Her hair was thick and black, settled luxuriously on her shoulders. One cheek showed the last traces of a bruise, a slight yellow tinge below her eye.

"Soon it's time to leave," she said. She had a battered suede handbag with her, fumbled in it for cigarettes.

The highway curved, went up and down like a roller coaster. Moments when the sky was grey the pavement threatened to fade into it. But when the sun was out it looked absurd, a narrow strip winding through forest and marsh, going nowhere.

Eventually they came to a dirt-road turn-off, the same road C.W. had gone down with the government men. Now it was improved and smoother. The boy drove the hearse slowly, the crates of dynamite in the back bouncing with each rut and pothole. At the old camp there was a group of men sitting around a picnic table. The explosives shack had a new door and there were new machines parked in a jumble through the clear area.

On the table they had more maps, a kettle full of coffee, small cardboard boxes full of food. The foreman's map was the same as C.W.'s. But his wheel was drawn in black pencil, the spokes thick and heavy. As soon as the boy got out the foreman left the table and looked in the back of the hearse, checking that everything was there.

"Goddam C.W.," the foreman said. "I never thought he would do anything like this." He laughed. He was a stocky man, almost fat, wearing the inevitable green quilted vest, and the company's special hardhat, a white plastic helmet with a decal of a treasure chest. He opened the back of the hearse and stacked the wooden crates on the ground, throwing them carelessly one on top of the other.

On one side of the clearing was a huge pile of lumber for the new dining hall and office. The cinder block foundation was already laid and beside it, the cedar planks looked raw and alive, fresh-cut and needing to be assembled before they started to warp.

The foreman returned to his table and the boy went to one of the bulldozers that was poised at the beginning of a new road. On one tread was his toolbox, wrapped in plastic to protect it against the rain. He opened it up and searched for the wrench he needed. When the transmission was apart and in front of him, the afternoon had passed. His hands and forearms were covered with grease, hair and needles matted indistinctly together. The sounds of chain saws had stopped but he could hear periodic shouts and explosions, imagine the shattered stumps floating high into the air.

Mary Gail was waiting for him, sitting so still and so silent she might have been there, behind, waiting the whole afternoon. She led him away from the camp and the explosions, down a long crescent trail that came out at the lake. He sat on a rock by the shore, lit a cigarette and smoked it slowly. It was only when he stood up to throw the butt into the water that he noticed the clearing and the remains of the village. On C.W.'s map, the village had been only a mark and a name, the place where one of the roads would have to end. But walking back into it from the shore it was more a feeling than a place, something old and strange that seemed to enter his bones as he came near. There was a huge hollow in the ground; crumbled logs surrounded it. Off to one side was an immense stump. At its base was a pile of bones, bleached narrow deer bones, as if a whole herd had perished.

The trees here were ancient. They stretched up to narrow green points in the sky. He walked around the inside circle of the trees. It was when he was almost back to where he had begun, back of where he had been sitting looking out at the lake, that he came across the mortuary poles, thick wide poles as high as a man could reach, crossed by the remains of a hollowed-out coffin. At the base of the poles was a mound. Mary Gail was standing beside it.

"My father's buried here," she said. As she spoke there was a short series of explosions. The boy looked towards the camp. On C.W.'s map the line had extended from the camp to the water. He wondered how many of these trees it would take to fill a boat.

C.W. locked his office and went out of the front door of the hotel. He looked up at his sign and then walked round to the parking lot. He had expected to find the hearse there but now, seeing that it was gone, remembered that the boy had taken it to the camp. He kept walking, his fast long stride quickly bringing him to the edge of town, to an unused dirt road than ran into an old logging territory.

Though the road had only been a path bulldozed and then covered with gravel, it hadn't grassed-over at all, only rutted and fallen away at the edges from the occasional use and the never-ending rain. On either side of the road, stretching to the hills on either side, was a tangle of bushes and vines that had grown up after the trees were removed, green bushes and vines pushing through the dead branches and limbs that had been too small or too difficult to drag out. There were some new trees too, the odd spruce or cedar, but they weren't very high.

Beneath his left arm C.W. carried a rifle, his smallest rifle, a .22 that fired long cartridges. He had read in the magazines that they had developed new weapons for the war in Asia, light rifles that fired with more impact, bullets that exploded whatever they touched. The newsreels from Vietnam showed the taped and broken bodies. And jungle trails filled with shit-smeared stakes, burnt-out fields and villages, bombed roads with every ditch a grave.

There was a thin mist over the road and the slash. It settled on his heavy leather walking boots, the striped pants he had carefully tucked into them, the old khaki parka he had brought up from Montana, his only relic from his days in the airforce. Its huge pockets flapped at his side, each filled with shells.

He walked for two miles, until he had worked his way to the top of a hill. He could see the town and the inlet that snaked into it from the sea. In one of his pockets he had, in addition to his shells, a thick brown envelope from his wife. He opened it up and photographs spilled to the ground, shiny-surfaced Polaroid photographs of her cats.

> . . . *who I began to see twice a week. For a long time I talked only about myself and about my own problems but eventually I began to talk about our marriage and to see that everything was not as it might be between us, Charles. One time, on my way to see him, the car broke down, and I had to take a taxi. He offered to drive me home as I was the last appointment, and I accepted.*
>
> *I know the details would only cause you great pain so I will skip over them except to say that I know a special place in my heart is reserved for you and all the wonderful things we shared.*
>
> *In the spring we'll get married in the town where his parents live. It's a nice little place near the border with a small wooden church, and, if it turns out I'm too old to start a family, I think we'll adopt children.*
>
> *The lawyer will tell you the rest. I hope you don't*

mind who I choose, I thought you might feel better if it was
someone you didn't know.
The basement is still leaking so I am having a new
sump. . . .

C.W. carefully arranged the photographs into walls,
then folded the letter in half so it sat on top of them, a high
white peaked roof. He tried to remember when he had last
written to her. On their wedding night she had cried and
bled on the white starched sheets. He had bought her
flowers the next day but it was already too late.

He couldn't remember very much about the honeymoon; it had all melted in with the jokes he had heard
about disastrous first weeks and estranged couples, with the
sausage-like actors writhing together in the stag movies his
friends had shown him the night before the wedding.

C.W. made small adjustments on his paper and
celluloid house, then paced off a hundred feet. He lay down
on the wet road, his elbows and the rifle forming a careful
triangle. He aimed at the front wall and squeezed the
trigger. The house fell down. He pulled five shells from his
pocket and shot each of them at the pile, each shot sending
up bits of white and dirt. When he was finished he went
back, searched for the remains and burned them. He felt
silly and foolish. He decided he would write to her and say
that she could have the house and the car.

He heard a movement in the slash. In the small valley
below him one deer had chased another out into the open.
They stopped and looked around. He was sitting down, the
wind blowing into him. Through his sights the deer's head
looked like a toy, still and brown. As he squeezed the trigger
he unaccountably moved the rifle, jerking it up into the air.
The deer, startled by the sound of the shot, took off across
the valley, disappeared quickly.

Among his father's set of The World's Greatest Books

had been some volumes on religion. One night, after supper, he had come upstairs from the basement and called the family together.

"The physical world is an illusion," C.W.'s father had said.

Everyone had waited patiently for him to finish so they could go back to their work.

"This house isn't here," C.W.'s father had said. "It only seems to be here because we are ignorant."

"That's nice," C.W.'s mother had said. During the day he ran the feed business but after dark he was known to be unreliable.

"The unexamined life is not worth living," C.W.'s father said. He went back down the basement.

In the dream he was running wildly through a field, his hands held to his ears. A dog was falling from the sky. He put down his rifle, unzipped his parka to the wet wind. He put the rifle and the boxes of shells under a limb, then started walking again, away from the town.

When he came back to retrieve the rifle and the shells it was getting dark. At the hotel he stood in his shower for a long time, the water scalding through his hair and his beard, edging around the still-swollen lump on his lower lip. He wondered what was wrong with him, letting the rifle get wet, missing the deer, letting that old drunk Johnny Tulip make a fool of him in front of Mary Gail.

And by the end of the night, two o'clock in the morning when the bar was closed and clean and it was time to go to bed, he remembered only two things: the bottle of scotch and the lock on his door.

Twelve

The second snow was more impressive. It had started, slow and hesitant, just before they went to sleep. But by the time Laurel Hobson woke up there were several inches of it on the ground, wet and porous. The blue sky and the bright sun made it look like white icing spread insanely on the floor of the forest, hanging in layers from the trees and bushes, edged around the bottom of their roof.

These days she woke up with her mind in her stomach, trying to keep it down. Her senses had turned inside out, betrayed her, transformed the world into a conspiracy of offensive smells, jolts, innumerable and unpredictable threats to whatever it was that had previously kept her food in its place, let it pass unthinkingly through her stomach.

She had gone finally, on Calvin's insistence and her own curiosity, to the doctor. His wife was back, sitting at the desk in the centre hall of the clinic. She was tinier than ever, so small that if she shrunk further she would have to start sitting on telephone books. "Hello dear," she said, her smile wide and different too, obviously pleased with herself. She was wearing a big new ring on her wedding finger, a band of silver encrusted with a row of three large emeralds. She escorted Laurel to the doctor's office, stayed while he examined her and gave her a bottle to pee in.

When he had inspected her insides he checked her

heart too, sliding the stethoscope into her unbuttoned shirt, cold round metal on her skin, a smooth steel fish. He tapped and closed his eyes. Then he asked her to take off her shirt. His wife stood beside her and slipped a hospital gown over her shoulders. The fish swam over her back, in between her ribs.

"You're supposed to stop smoking," the doctor said. Tap tap. Now that his wife was back, it turned out that his voice was loud all the time, loud and embarrassed, as if he was practising talking in front of a mirror.

"I better cut down," Laurel said.

"It makes your baby smaller," the doctor said. The steel fish was growing warm. In some places she felt more hollow than others.

"You don't want a fat baby," the doctor's wife said practically. "The fatter it is, the harder it is to get it out." She giggled.

"Women should have their babies squatting," the doctor said. He was still standing behind Laurel, tapping and listening. His wife was standing in front of her. Laurel could smell peppermints on her breath. The doctor's wife was getting tired, her arms holding the gown up over Laurel's front.

"Is this your first?"

Laurel nodded.

"You see," she said to her husband. "She better have a small one."

"It's just the size of the head that matters," the doctor said. He took away his stethoscope and stepped back. The doctor's wife dropped the gown. They were both looking at her breasts. Laurel looked down. They seemed pretty ordinary to her. She put on her shirt.

"Excuse me," she said, "where's the bathroom?" On her knees as soon as the door was locked. Her stomach contracted into a knot and then sprang loose.

No cramps that day, her second period missed, no sign of anything leaving except up through her throat.

"Come back in a month," the doctor said. Standing by the window, trying to crack his knuckles through the rubber gloves.

His wife led her to the desk, gave her the forms to sign. She sat down in her chair while Laurel printed out the particulars. The doctor had gone back into his office. His wife took a package of peppermint candies out of her white coat, a white linen coat that was pressed and shaped, better material than the doctor's. "Miss Hobson," she whispered. Her voice was tiny but distant.

"Yes?"

"Is he going to marry you?"

Laurel was busily printing out her aunt's address in the section for next-of-kin.

"Is he?" She was still whispering.

"I don't remember who it was," Laurel said.

"Well." There was a long pause. She inspected Laurel's face carefully, looking at it with the same care she had shown before. Then she looked down at the form, saw that the aunt's name was Hobson too. "You shouldn't make jokes like that."

"I'm sorry," she said. "I must have been drunk."

And at night Laurel had dreamed the afternoon over. So going out now into the snow to empty the basin she almost expected to see the doctor and his wife plodding slowly up the beach, wearing buckled city galoshes and carrying pads of paper and pencils, ready to interrogate her again, collect the rent.

Coming back in she started the fire and shoved the kettle over it. Then settled into the couch and lit a cigarette, smoke to steady her stomach, initiate the day.

L-A-U-R-E-L (six letters): a salmon that has spent the

summer in fresh water; also, an evergreen shrub of the mediterranean region with aromatic, lance-shaped leaves. By afternoon most of the snow was gone. Just a few traces here in town where Laurel waited in the truck, finishing her crossword, while Calvin negotiated the liquor store.

Johnny at the window, his face pale and exhausted. There were pouches under his eyes, the skin was bagged and purple. He climbed in the truck, driver's side, slammed the door. She felt herself pushing away the noise, the inevitable disasters that he would draw her into. Already he was looking studiously down at his hands, rolling a cigarette.

"You look sick," Johnny said. Laurel realized she was hunched over in the seat, one hand on her stomach and the other on her newspaper.

"It's just my stomach," Laurel said. It was only three weeks since she had seen him, the day Mary Gail was in the clinic.

"I heard you were in town yesterday," Johnny said. "I was out hunting." But he looked as if he had been lying in someone's basement. His hands were shaking and his nose seemed to have broken out in a maze of tiny veins. He coughed and hit his hand against his chest.

"Cold winter," Laurel said. "Snow so early."

"My mother said that it will be warm at Christmas." Johnny coughed again. The cigarette seemed tiny and lost; his face was too big for cigarettes. He lit the cigarette and the smell of the sulphur from the match cut through her throat.

"You shouldn't inhale from the match," Laurel said.

"What?"

"The match is the worst part," Laurel said. "People in match factories die from them all the time. Really."

"Jesus," Johnny Tulip said. His cigarette had gone out and he had to light it again. He inhaled with the match at its tip but this time didn't cough, only swallowed and made a face.

"It tastes awful," he admitted. His voice today so broken, like a motor gone dry and turned in on itself.

Calvin came out, saw Johnny in the truck, waved and went down the street towards the grocery store.

In her dream the doctor and his wife had looked not like they were supposed to, but like William-and-Mary. And it had taken place not in the clinic but in a vast thick-carpeted living-room, with a fireplace at one end and islands of furniture and coffee tables scattered between the wall with the fireplace and the huge picture window which looked out on a long formal garden leading down to the sea.

"We only want what's best for you," William Hobson had said. He was dressed in a suit of maps, continents gliding off his arms and shoulders, a big inland lake tied carefully around his neck. The living-room was entirely empty except for the three of them.

"Yes," Mary Hobson echoed. "We only want what's best for you."

William Hobson's costume shimmered and dissolved into doctor's whites. A lamp appeared in his hand. He pointed it at his own face. Mary Hobson held up a mirror.

"There," she said. "There and there." Her finger touched the three separate spots: one on William Hobson's forehead, and one on each of his cheeks. Laurel couldn't see anything special about them.

"And now you too," Mary Hobson said, pointing at Laurel. Both Mary Hobson and Laurel were wearing whites too, coats but no pants.

"Oh for God's sake," William Hobson said. He went to a wall and pulled down a screen. The lights went off and he picked up a microphone. Flashes of colour appeared, then numbers.

"We wanted you to see this when your time came,"

William Hobson said. "So you would know what we went through to have you."

The numbers were rapidly descending. A round zero filled the screen. It was red and blue. A pause and the screen went blank. A huge belly gradually emerged. Smooth and female, long stretch marks on either side. The camera moved back. It was Mary Hobson, pregnant and wearing a two-piece sunsuit, eating a popsicle. Laurel started to laugh.

"Stop that," William Hobson said.

But Mary Hobson was laughing too, a high shrill laugh that Laurel had never heard before. Mary Hobson stepped up to the screen with a long wooden ruler. She waved it at the image of herself. It was replaced by a film of William Hobson riding a bicycle around a circular track, faster and faster, speeded up and wavering.

"I bet you didn't know your father could do that," Mary Hobson said. The bicycle blurred. The screen began to burn.

She knew she was dreaming. She tried to wake herself up. She opened her eyes and found she was lying on one of the couches. The room was empty. The screen had fallen off the wall and was lying in charred bits on the floor. The furniture was all battered and broken, the upholstery torn open and wads of foam stuffing scattered about the carpet. She looked for William-and-Mary but didn't see them. She was dressed normally again, in her jeans and her shirt. Wandering about the wreckage of the room, she saw that a table had been brought in, a metal table on wheels, and placed against one wall. It was covered with a cloth. She lifted it up. There were trays of medical instruments and bottles.

She put the cloth back and went to the window. The garden was green and glittering. Fountains sprayed up into the air. The sea was calm, green too, a deep glassed-over green that didn't move at all.

172

There were groups of people sitting at tables in the garden, talking and drinking tea. Over each table was a striped umbrella. She stepped outside, passing through the window and onto the lawn as easily as she thought it, instantly warmed and calmed by the hot sun and the smell of grass and flowers.

She sat with William and Mary. There were small trays of elaborately iced cakes in the centre of the round table, trays like the ones she had seen inside. One of the cakes had an L printed on the top, made out of small silver candies. She bit into it. The cake tasted sweet and metallic, stuck to her lips and tongue.

"That's better," Mary said.

"Yes," William said. "That's better." In the breast pocket of his white coat were his lamp and his mirror.

"We didn't want you to miss the show," Mary said. The tables were arranged so that they all faced an empty space of lawn backed by flowers and shrubs.

"You can't see it yet," William said. "They're not here." He shone his lamp uselessly around the lawn.

From somewhere there was music. She understood there was a band. She stood up, hoping to find something to drink. The people at the tables seemed familiar but she couldn't quite recognize any of them. Finally she came to the place where Johnny and Victoria were sitting. They had a big-bellied silver teapot in the middle of their table. Laurel sat down.

Johnny and Victoria had been talking to one another. Now they stopped. Victoria looked at Laurel. Her face glistened with the heat. She was wearing rings. "Well," Victoria said. She laughed. Her rings flashed in the sun. The music was louder now, brass and drums marching furiously up the hill. Victoria had been stiff and cold, swollen and frozen from the sea. Now she was still slow, all her gestures theatrical and exaggerated.

"It's all right," Victoria said. Her hands flashed across

the table and captured one of Laurel's. She held it closely cold and tight.

"I'm sorry," Laurel said. She felt besieged. She thought she could sense Johnny's leg under the table, searching for her's. She wriggled uncomfortably in her chair.

She looked back at Victoria. Victoria's face had started to waver, flashed glimpses of a raven's mask, of a fish in dark water.

Laurel felt cold all over, cold and stiff, cold the way Victoria must have felt when the alcohol wore off and she found herself numb and kicking in the ocean, her lungs full of water and salt, her legs wrapped round and bound in weeds and kelp. The only place that wasn't cold was deep down in her belly, the lump-sized child turning her guts inside out to greet Victoria, sucking in all her heat in one tremendous breath that threatened to collapse the whole afternoon, swallow everything, even the band, which was now assembled in the cusp of the garden, uniforms red and blue. Blue to match the colour of their eyes, blue eyes like William Hobson's, red to match the doll's spots painted once on each cheek and once on the forehead.

The sun was in her eyes. Squinting and leaning forward she could see the band more clearly. The leader turned to her. He too had blue eyes, red doll's spots on his face. In the front pocket of his uniform he had a small mirror. He waved his arms, the motions stiff and precise. The band burst into a floor of sound. William Hobson, strutting back and forth, urging on the band. And every player the same, every one tall and bony, sleepily blasting apart the afternoon.

She looked for Johnny and Victoria. They had left the table. Then she saw them at the edge of the garden, running. Her insides reached out for them, breathed again. Her stomach started to convulse. She woke up with her feet already slapping against the cold floor, stumbling into the

174

living-room of the cabin: morning, the snow wet and porous on the ground, bits of the dream still clinging to her as
she stood at the window, seeing the snow, the blue sky and
the bright sun making it look like white icing spread insanely on the floor of the forest, hanging in layers from the trees
and bushes, edged around the bottom of their roof.

"It tastes awful," Johnny admitted. The match held to the
tip of his cigarette. His voice today so broken, a motor gone
dry and turned in on itself.

Calvin came out, saw Johnny in the truck, waved and
went down the street towards the grocery store.

"I dreamed about you last night," Laurel said.

Johnny pushed the match into the ashtray, poked a
hole for it among the overflowing butts and ashes.

In the dream his skin had been smooth and young, like
Victoria's, soft copper skin stretched over his bones. Today
his face looked like it was made out of a hide, weathered and
crusted. Even in three weeks his hair had turned greyer.
Soon he would be an old man. Soon someone would come
up the beach to tell her that he was dead. The flesh on his
hips had been shiny and deep, cold in her hands, slippery as
milk.

She pushed the newspaper away from her. "I wish
Calvin would come back," Laurel said. "We could go for a
coffee."

Johnny coughed and hit his chest.

She saw his lips were loose and red. She could tell he
was breathing carefully, trying to ease the air over the spots
that hurt. Soon she would be afraid to see him. He opened
the window and spat out onto the street. She wanted to
touch him but didn't want him to feel her pity.

"We can tell him in the store," Laurel said. Pushing
open her door and standing on the street. Picking her way

through the slush and puddles to the sidewalk. Johnny Tulip stood beside her. His hair was thinner and greyer. Through it she could see signs of his scalp.

"Come on," Johnny said. This sidewalk had been a government project three summers ago, something to give the Indians work during a slack fishing season. The arrangement had been that the workers would be paid, rain or shine. But when it rained, it was impossible to mix concrete. So the sidewalk extended about a hundred yards, connecting the liquor store and the grocery store, along with a defunct bowling alley, a building that had once been a community hall and was now boarded up, and several vacant lots.

They moved slowly along the sidewalk, their arms linked, looking down, matching their steps. Johnny Tulip was wearing old leather shoes, black patent leather that was wrinkled and soaked through. With each step they could hear the squish of the water inside. The sound made Laurel's own feet feel wet. She wriggled her toes against each other.

The grocery had been modernized: its original wooden doors were replaced now by glass ones. Laurel pushed Johnny into the store ahead of her, marched him down to the back where there was an assortment of lumber jackets, jeans, long underwear and raingear. There was a chair there and she made Johnny sit down in it. Picked out a pair of boots and socks and stood over him while he tried them on. Soon he would be too old for this. He would have to spend the winters inside.

"You goddamn idiot," Laurel said. "What do you think you're doing?" His feet were red and covered with blisters and sores. So cold they were shaking and he had to press them, one by one, to the floor, keeping the heel down so he could get the socks hooked over his toes.

Calvin was standing at the end of the aisle with a shopping cart partly filled with tins and boxes. He was holding a package in his hand totally absorbed in reading the directions. They ended up, the three of them, standing at the cash desk. Laurel, with her unemployment cheque, paid for everything.

They drove Johnny Tulip home. In the summer his mother's house was light grey, cedar-weathered and bleached by the sun. But the weeks of constant rain had soaked the wood and stained it dark. It would stay this way, black and wet, until next summer. The house and the kitchen smelled. Johnny's mother was away, visiting someone at the other end of the village. There were store cookies and white bread and jam scattered over the kitchen table. The living-room was quiet and strangely still. The curtains were closed. Nothing was visible except the round cedar coffee table that Harry Jones had made for his wife, a gleaming cedar table that had been fitted together by hand and rubbed with linseed oil until it shone.

They started a fire and made tea when the water boiled. In the dream there had been a silver teapot, but she couldn't remember drinking anything. On the kitchen wall was a faded newspaper photograph of Victoria sitting on the front verandah. It had been newer then, none of the posts sagged. The picture had been taken by a Vancouver reporter who had come up to do a story on one of Canada's last and proudest Indian tribes. In the picture Victoria was identified, incorrectly, as the island's "pretty young native schoolteacher." In fact she had never gone to school, and didn't even learn to read until one day, when her mother dragged her to church, she heard the minister give a sermon warning against the evils of pornographic literature.

Laurel sipped at her tea, watched Johnny and Calvin make sandwiches out of the white bread. The house seemed damp, as if the fire was lit only sporadically. She took a small piece of bread and covered it with butter and jam. It tasted sticky and sweet, too sweet, making her teeth feel hollow and vulnerable. An oilcloth was tacked to the table. She found a rag by the sink and wiped off the space in front of her. The rag smelled sour and old. She threw it back into the sink, wiped her hands on her jeans.

She felt in a stupor. It always seemed that way, as winter set in. She couldn't remember the last time the sun had shone all day, that she had spent the whole day outside. In the dream she had wanted Victoria to forgive her. She pressed her hand to her stomach. She didn't feel nauseous any more, only depressed and hemmed in by the prospect of endless clouds and rain. In the bottom of her cup were tiny remnants of tea. Johnny and Mary Gail went around the island every summer, gathering various kinds of leaves, and bringing them home to hang upside down by the stove. Then they mixed them together: mint, raspberry, dandelion, alfalfa—leaves she didn't even recognize—and put them in glass jars for the winter.

It was when they were on the verge of leaving that Mary Gail came downstairs, walking stiffly down the narrow staircase that was on the far side of the living-room, then limping into the kitchen. Her face was pallid, her hair stringy and unkempt. Above one eye she had been cut. There was a bandage and her forehead was swollen unevenly. She sat down heavily at the table, then had to get up to rinse herself out a cup. Her knuckles were bruised and scraped.

"She looks bad," Johnny said. "But you should see her room at the hotel."

Mary Gail smiled. She loaded up her tea with heaping spoons of sugar and poured in canned milk. She was sitting beside Laurel and put her hand on Laurel's arm. "I don't know what's wrong with me," she said. "I get so mad at men."

Johnny coughed.

"Well," Mary Gail admitted, "he wasn't there. I got the axe from the hall and just went crazy I guess." She shook her head.

Laurel looked at her but couldn't see anything in her face that showed her anger. She remembered that the week she had stayed there, Mary Gail had started a fight with one of Victoria's boy-friends. He had refused to let her drive his car so finally Mary Gail had put a rock through its windshield.

"I never really remember anything," she said. "It all goes fuzzy and blank."

The tea had been made in an extraordinarily ugly pot that was the family favourite, a high oval-bellied brown pot with two yellow canaries painted on each side. Laurel poured herself more tea, watched the canaries dip and bob their heads. Mary Gail's hand was still on her arm. Her fingers were short and like a girl's, the nails all bitten down.

In the dream she had been sitting at the table with Johnny and Victoria, about to drink tea, and now she wondered if this was what the dream was prophesying, with Mary Gail playing the part of her dead sister and Calvin, tall and bony, his face frozen with polite discomfort, standing in for William-and-Mary, the band, the living-room with its islands of furniture and its large square window looking vacantly out to the garden. Beside Johnny, Calvin appeared curiously young and anonymous, his thick hair and close-shaven skin placing him in another world, a manicured world that would have been familiar to William Hobson, where people avoided using themselves up and lasted a long time. Except, of course, for accidents. She hadn't seen the remnants of the car. Only an item on the accountant's statement: fifteen dollars from the wrecker. But even smashed and crumpled the car would have been clean, a baby blue Chevrolet that William Hobson washed and polished every week, the seats covered with shiny clear plastic.

"Come on," Mary Gail said, "I have to show you something." Her fingers tightened on Laurel's arm and then released. Laurel followed Mary Gail, out of the kitchen and into the living-room which was dark and always vaguely eerie to her, room of a blind person, Johnny Tulip's mother always sitting in the same place, a wicker rocking chair behind the round table Harry Jones had made for her. Then up the narrow stairs, holding carefully to the shaky bannister, avoiding bits and pieces of clothes, tools, old newspapers.

Each zone of this house had its own odour. The kitchen was a mixture of woodsmoke and sour food smells. The living-room was stale and damp, tinged with strange incense that Johnny's mother sometimes burned. Laurel had never even been upstairs before. Clothes spilled out of broken dressers and cardboard boxes. One room had its door closed. She wondered if that was where Victoria had slept, if they had come home from the funeral and just shut the door, like that. The way her aunt would have done on William-and-Mary.

Mary Gail's room smelled musty and unused. The stovepipe from the kitchen reappeared in its centre, rising through a pile of clothes and then making a right-angle turn to bury itself in a small rusted oil drum that was stuck through the wall. The pipe was layered with innumerable streaks of tar and resin, run-off from the alder and spruce they used here.

The bed was on the floor, just a mattress, but covered with spectacularly new sheets, linen sheets with huge red roses, and, of course, a pillowcase to match. Mary Gail sat down on the bed, crossed her legs. Laurel sat down beside her. Once half the window had been broken. The gap was plugged by a piece of cardboard, taped to the remaining glass. The cardboard was stained and warped from years of rains.

"Well," Mary Gail said. She leaned over and shuffled around in her clothes until she found a package of cigarettes and a plastic bag of her mother's home-grown marijuana. She lit a cigarette and then, with it in her mouth and her eyes squinted shut to avoid the smoke, stuffed some of the marijuana into a small pipe. She held a match to it, sucked in sharply, then passed it to Laurel. In her mysterious way, Johnny Tulip's mother was able to garden blind. Laurel had seen her, on her knees in the back yard; testing the flowers and weeds with her hands, pulling out what didn't belong and propping up what did.

"It's not bad," Mary Gail said. "But not like the other." Meaning the winter Johnny had brought up an impossibly huge amount of cocaine from Vancouver and he and Laurel and Mary Gail had spent weeks in Laurel's cabin, getting high and sleeping, until finally their accelerating appetite had wiped out their supply, and they had emerged into the normal world, gaunt and strung-out. So desperate for money then, and upset that winter hadn't yet turned into spring, Laurel had written to her aunt. And her aunt had written back saying that if she wanted to come and live with her in Vancouver, she could have room and board for only ten dollars a week.

In the dream there had been no drugs at all, only William Hobson with his lamp and fastidious mirror, his tray of discreetly covered instruments. But when she had accepted her aunt's offer, and the enclosed ticket, the winter had grown farther away. Had dissolved into a haze of alcohol and morphine, microscopic moments of a flashed glimpse of her own skin, of herself kneeling on the floor of her room at her aunt's house, bending over, solid gold growing out of her belly.

Mary Gail was holding out a dark blue velvet box. In the box, mounted on a small white satin post, was a ring. The ring was narrow and gold with a bulge on the top. Seated on the bulge, grasped in a hollow silver flower, was a huge diamond. Laurel took the box, brought it closer to her face. The diamond had a million facets, seemed as big as a strawberry, perfectly sharp at each corner and perfectly flat on each plane, the ugliest thing she had ever seen.

"Isn't that fantastic?" Mary Gail's face registered shock, as if she was seeing it for the first time. Her face seemed awkward and shiny. "Isn't it?"

"Where did it come from?"

"I think C.W.'s wife sent it to him," Mary Gail said, whispering confidentially. She giggled. Laurel laughed too. Her voice seemed to have detached itself, bounced out of her chest in long bright stripes. The pipe was hot against her lips. She formed them into an O, poked out rings of smoke with her tongue. In Vancouver she had lost track of everything. Spent the days standing like a zombie in front of a supermarket cash-register, banging the keys, drinking and smoking at night. Sleeping in long transparent stretches, sleeps that penetrated into waking, veiled and protected her as she punched out the numbers, stuffed food into bags and boxes.

Mary Gail took the pipe from Laurel's hand. Laurel exhaled slowly. The smoke drifted aimlessly in the air. Laurel closed her eyes.

"I feel like I'm in a room," Laurel said. She meant aquarium but couldn't locate the right word for water.

"A room," Mary Gail repeated. "That's possible."

"Room," Laurel said. The vowels swam in her head. She imagined her lf reading the London telephone directory, each name rushing through the tunnel. She felt like she was swimming. The room was filled with chaotic lines of force, strung in bunches, magnetic ropes knotted and tangled hopelessly together. She shrugged, trying to straighten them out. She waved her hands. She was swimming through a slow grey mass. It was an eye. Light came in but she couldn't see out.

"Laurel."

In the dream William Hobson had wanted her to use the mirror too. He had held the lamp out for her, shone it in her face.

One time she had passed out during dinner. Her aunt dragged her into the living-room and put her on the couch. When she came out of it her aunt was so pleased, she gave her a glass of sherry.

"Laurel." She couldn't see anything. "Laurel are you all right?"

"Just tired," Laurel said. She felt for the wall and turned so she was leaning against it. She drew her knees into her stomach. The eye was suspended in a fish lying just below the surface of the water. She floated through it. Mary Gail's hand was on her head now, twined into the hair at the back of her neck, strong and human. Laurel could see the bitten fingers pushing into her neck, sliding against her scalp.

"Johnny says you're pregnant." She floated but there was no sense of where it might end. She wondered how those who had eyes could see, when the eyes themselves were blind. In the dream Victoria had refused to look at her. There had been three chairs at the table and a huge silver teapot. Victoria had only looked at Johnny. Or across the lawn to where the band was coming. Even in the dream she had been dead.

"I hope you stay and have the baby on the island." Mary Gail sounded suddenly like Louise, her voice high and sincere. The eye was a giant round room. The lines of force ran in knotted ropes from the front to the back. They didn't focus anywhere, only passed through on their way to some imaginary destination.

She shifted against the wall. It was as liquid and uncertain as her back. The fish quivered and Laurel was floating again, swimming lost in the eye. The grey was broken up and patchy, like a sky on a cloudy day.

She folded her arms tightly across her chest, slowed down. She was rocking back and forth. Mary Gail's hand was still on her neck, probing, deeper than Calvin, stripping away layers of flesh and muscle, the fingers finding the spine, the hollow core of nerves and signals.

"That feels good," Laurel said.

"Johnny used to rub my neck when I was sick." William Hobson had never been sick. Only exhausted, crawling about on his study floor, assembling huge composite maps that he had sketched himself, trying to come out with the same picture as the atlas. Mary Gail's hand slid down her back, found the place where the bone had been cracked, pushed against it, like a button, releasing warmth everywhere, flooding her, her eyes and nose suddenly full and warm. William Hobson never cried. His eyes were small and dry. Being inside them would be like being buried in sand. At least this eye was wet and whole. But even a fish could see, respond to colour and movement. Mary Gail's hand was light on her spine. The nerves rippled and jumped to meet the pressure of her fingers. Once Johnny had told Laurel how to catch salmon by hand: kneel in the shade beside a good fast stream, find a quiet pocket, a fat salmon hovering near the bank, then slowly immerse a hand in the water just above the tail fins, tickle the water, run the hand up the back of the salmon, slowly, mesmerizing it, then straighten the two big fingers into a V and plunge them down into the water, hooking the salmon behind the gills and flipping it onto the bank. Not an easy trick, Johnny admitted, but the bears do it. William Hobson didn't. He fished with a rod and a red and silver spinner, caught small cut-throat trout and fried them over a fire, in his special pan with a collapsible handle.

The eye was a sphere floating slow and dizzy. Not in this room, she was anchored here by the floor and Mary Gail's hand, but somewhere else that existed in the same place, ran through it in endless convoluted tunnels.

"I wanted to show you the ring," Mary Gail said. "Because C.W. gave it to me and he wants me to marry him."

"God," Laurel said.

Mary Gail giggled. "I know it's crazy. I was so mad when he gave it to me, I almost killed myself." She took her hand away. There was the sound of tinfoil rustling, a match being lit.

"You want one?"

The cigarette was fat and round in her fingers. She brought it towards her mouth. It was hot but her reactions were too slow. The burning tip brushed her chin as she turned it around. The filter fit into her mouth like a plug. The smoke was lukewarm and tasteless. She reached for an ashtray and found the bone pipe instead.

"C.W.," Laurel said. The initials sounded significant but the details escaped her.

Mary Gail giggled again. "Really," she said. "Imagine me, married. He said he'd buy me a house."

Laurel started to open her eyes but then was afraid. This view was better, grey and neutral.

"What did you tell him?"

Mary Gail's hand was back, this time on her knee. "Nothing. I just went up to my room and wrecked it."

William had proposed to Mary in a library. Just as she was about to refuse the librarian had asked them to leave.

On the way home he talked her into it. "The most important thing is that we're friends," Mary Hobson used to say. She would say this to Laurel while they were doing the dishes, the kitchen directly below William Hobson's study, the shuffle of papers and drawers occasionally audible through gaps in her story.

"I don't think my mother would like C.W.," Mary Gail said.

"No."

"It's easy for someone else to tell you what to do."

Johnny had come down to Vancouver in the spring. Laurel was still staying at her aunt's house, working at the supermarket, drinking sherry with her aunt after dinner. Johnny sat with them in the living-room, sipping as delicately as possible from one of the crystal glasses William-and-Mary had received for their wedding. Laurel's aunt put fresh sheets on the bed in the guest room. On the wall was one of Mary Hobson's needle-point maps, an indistinct and brightly coloured explosion that seemed like something seen through a microscope. And on the shelves were souvenirs William had collected: old arrowheads and flints, a bark replica of a canoe, a pair of elaborately beaded moccasins that were now dry and cracked, but once belonged to a real Indian chief.

When her aunt went to bed, Johnny and Laurel walked down to the beach. It was warm. There were still traces of sun in the sky, long red streaks racing hopelessly about the horizon. Johnny had more cocaine and a tiny silver spoon.

"It's bad luck to live in the city," Johnny said. Even then his voice had been broken and jagged. In the city his old serge suits and his huge uncivilized face looked only seedy and rundown. The same way she felt with her cupboard filled with empty bottles, her body so shot through with alcohol that there was nowhere for the cocaine to take hold. It spread out along the surface, like one of Mary Hobson's maps, like William Hobson's inland lake, spilling down his shirtfront.

"They used to think this was the edge of the world," Laurel said.

"Okay," Johnny said. "This is the edge of the world." He poked his hand into the sky, wriggled his fingers. In those days he used to sing while he played, the noise from his throat so unexpected it sounded as if the piano was defective.

Then he had started talking about his mother, the long dead boat rides to and from Vancouver. While he told her about the operation and the missionaries' houses, she couldn't see anything but his mother's eyes, swollen and useless, broken open by white blood.

And at the end of the night her nerves were empty. She could only lie helplessly on the beach, face down, every available atom pressed into the sand, wanting him but unable to say anything or move.

In the dream no one had touched. Now she felt encased in skin, wrapped up and held. She wondered if this was what it was like to be an embryo fastened to the side of the womb, an eye cupped into skin and fat. She could feel Mary Gail's hand through her shirt, drawing sweat out of her back and shoulders, soaking her, circling in a thin ring around the waist of her jeans.

She tried to imagine Mary Gail getting married to C.W. They would move to an adjoining suite, spend their honeymoon in a hotel in Vancouver. Mary Gail would order breakfast in bed, hot chocolate and pancakes. She would buy new clothes and make C.W. take her to the movies.

"Laurel?"

"Okay," Laurel said. "I have to see the ring again." She was still leaning against the wall but her position had become awkward and unbalanced. She tried to force some

187

sort of sensation through her muscles. She put her hands down and tested them against the bed. The woollen blanket was rough to the touch. She felt it suddenly, a long scream starting deep in her belly, pushing out uninterrupted in every direction until her stomach and chest were absolutely empty of air, pushed in on themselves. So dry and locked up inside, muscles crammed and fighting for air. Mary Gail's fingers like irons across her neck, burning her open.

Finally she would walk up the beach with Calvin. He would be carrying the groceries in a cardboard box, walking quickly with their weight, his boots digging deep into the sand. They would get to a place where the highway and the truck were out of sight, the town and the logging camp inaudible. There would be only beach and cliffs and ocean. The hawks and gulls would be indistinct against the grey sky, but their cries would ride easily above the noise of the waves and wind. They would stop and sit on a log, looking out at the ocean. When they got to the cabin it would be cold and indifferent. Warm, it would be theirs again. In the morning winter would be one day closer, the floor frozen against her bare feet, the frozen cedar splitting easy and glass-like, long pink splinters spread out like petals in the snow.

From the window of Mary Gail's room, the truck looked absurd and small. Its red roof was uneven and rusted. Chunks of wood were piled in the back and there was a piece of canvas inaccurately thrown over a chainsaw. On the other side of the street, the ground sloped down towards the cove. She could see over and between the opposing houses, down to where the few boats that remained to the Indians were moored to a new government dock. One totem pole was visible, its paint long gone, staring squat and bored across the water.

There were no people on the street. Only a scattering of dogs, garbage, and derelict vehicles. When it was dark the yellow government school bus would come, the houses would open up with noise and slamming doors.

In her palm Laurel held C.W.'s ring. The diamond was cold and sharp, something that should be kept at a distance. Its light had traces of blue and red. It reminded her of cutting instruments and drills.

She tried to put on the ring. C.W.'s wife must have had tiny hands. Perhaps they helped her to slide the cats in and out of cages. The ring fit only on Laurel's smallest finger, the last finger of her left hand. She pressed the diamond against the window. This could be the edge of the world: she drew an eye-shaped oval in the glass. In the middle of the eye she drew a circle. She bent down and looked through. The sky was broken and calm. Everything was the same. Across the street the door of the house opened. A woman emerged. She was carrying a bucket of garbage. She went around to the back of the house. When she came back she was wiping one hand against her skirt, swinging the empty bucket with the other. She saw Laurel watching her and grinned, her teeth white and gold.

"Well?" Mary Gail asked.

"I don't know," Laurel said. She was carefully scratching lashes on to the eyes. "He's still married, isn't he?"

"I tried to tell him that. He said I have to make up my mind, so he has something to believe in."

Laurel went back to the bed for a cigarette. Mary Gail was sitting on the mattress. Laurel knelt down in front of her. She could still hear her own voice. She reached out for Mary Gail. She looked like neither Johnny nor Victoria, only young and unaware, someone who didn't belong in the dream at all. Mary Gail's cheeks were flushed and warm against her hands. Laurel could feel her own face turning red and embarrassed. She bent her head down further. Mary Gail put her arms around her shoulders, drew her into her lap, her hands searing wherever they touched.

Even Mary Gail's jeans were hot, her thighs and belly burning through the denim, igniting the sudden and overwhelming odour of every man who had slept with her, more, Laurel realized, than she could ever know about, a vast collection of homeless flesh seeking and pouring membership and salvation into this one hole, leaving behind only this strange museum of smell and taste which she now felt pushed through like a reluctant tourist, needing it too, drinking it in like a long and musty sacramental wine, drunk and drowned, Victoria's ghost home cold.

Thirteen

This night was cold and clear. The waves collapsed slowly into the beach, sending long shallow pools of foam skidding across the sand, flat white mirrors in the light of the moon. December, and Orion and Sirius dominated the sky, ascending magically from the ocean even while signs of day remained.

It was low tide and the sand stretched far out from the cliffs. They walked where it was packed hard, their boots digging in and sucking the water out from beneath the surface, small sharp sounds that beat time for them as they made their way from the cabin to the road.

They wore new matching parkas, coloured bright on the outside and lined with thick artificial fur. Warm and dry, the man at the store had said. He had laid the coats across the counter: two nylon corpses, fresh out of their bags. The price was marked on Calvin's stiff arms and swollen hands, endless loads of wood brought in on the truck, piled high in the metal shed behind the store.

Calvin's arms still buzzed and rattled whenever he straightened his elbows. The foam slid about the beach in large erratic shapes, a slow-motion kaleidoscope that changed with each slow wave. There was no snow on the beach itself, but at the base of the cliffs, where the tide hadn't reached for a couple of days, there was a thin collar of white.

In his pocket Calvin kept the red stone he had found at the end of summer. Now it seemed smaller and more worn, a season of carrying fitting it to his thigh. When they turned off the beach and into the woods, the air changed too: here it was colder and more fragrant, stripped of salt and loaded up with the odours of evergreen trees: fir, cedar and spruce mixed together, sweet and pungent. It was a week since they had been out. But their path was marked for them anyway, deer and rabbits wearing through a narrow trail.

The weather had turned cold, hovering around freezing during the day, dropping lower at night. It had snowed twice more and though the snow was only light and thin, it stayed, a couple of inches scattered on the forest floor, edged between the leaves and needles, a thin layer spread over the clearings, covering what was small but leaving the grass sticking through the surface, still green and straight, each blade making its own small tunnel around itself.

Despite the cold and the snow, they were still working on the new logging roads, sending the spokes out from the hub of the camp, using dynamite where it was too slow or difficult for the bulldozers. They were working faster now, afraid of a bad winter, and sometimes in the early mornings, when he was walking on the beach, Calvin could hear the explosions, muffled by the distance and the trees so they were felt as much as heard, long pointless tremours that shook the whole island.

He was used to inland winters, where the cold was dry and pinched. His body was confused by this new kind of winter, by the erratic temperatures and wood-heated houses that froze tight in the mornings. It thawed only slowly as he moved back from the stove; so sometimes whole days were passed in gradually rotating in front of the fire. But the cold here was never dangerous or threatening, didn't seem to have diminished the forest or its constant wet growth. Even the moss was thriving in this winter, springing out green and thick from stumps and broken limbs, gulping rain and snow with equal ease, the wet fecund leaves always dripping and bright, inhumanly eager, like a Universal Venus to which anything might fall.

At the road it was darker. The truck was barely visible, a lumpish shadow pushing up into the night. Calvin wiped the snow off the windshield with the sleeve of his parka, snow slightly crusted with fine bits staying stuck to the glass. The motor hesitated, then whined and gained speed, catching on the first try. They had tried to economize on gloves. While the engine warmed up they shook their hands and slapped them together. The windshield wipers were frozen and Calvin had to go outside, tear the rubber off the glass. The road looked almost like the beach, irregular white pools formed by the snow.

The first few times he had driven in the truck it had seemed over-sized and grotesque, its stiff ancient body unequal to the durability of its motor, like an elephant with an artificial heart. Habit had made it normal. Over the torn holes in the seat, where the springs protruded, they had put layers of cardboard, and more cardboard in the places where the floor was missing, not so much to keep out the cold as to keep out the exhaust which, despite their best efforts, still found its way in somewhere and had to be let out the open windows. But these were only minor inconveniences, matters to be set beside the ever-present need for clutch fluid and the absent brakes as proof of the ultimate, if narrow, triumph of technology over this wild island; and it was true that once the truck was moving and the lights began to work, Calvin could see the asphalt tracks of other vehicles through the snow.

These mornings Calvin woke up fuzzy and reluctant, soaked in forgotten dreams. Gradually he would pull himself away from the impassive wall that seemed always to be the first sign of awareness; and he would begin to fit into his own body, moving from the centre to the warm gaps where he was joined to Laurel. When he opened his eyes they always faced the same memory: the space between the stovepipe and the window, empty now, but still signalling the bony ribcage of the deer, the feel of gristle against his teeth, the blue summer light of Johnny Tulip's birthday. And in the cold time it took him to get dressed and go outside, the night escaped him entirely, left him stranded in the wet shining green of the new spruce forest that closed tightly around the cabin. Three months now, and although in some way he was becoming used to the smells and the sounds, the place was still absolutely foreign to him, divided him from himself, the day from the night, the present from the past, with absolute finality, morning passed to evening without effort or remembrance.

"I like this," Laurel said, "driving at night in winter." The cold cut the smell of the fumes. Calvin rolled the window part-way up, drove faster to get more heat.

"We used to have relatives in Prince George," she said. "Sometimes we drove up there for Christmas." He tried to imagine that being pregnant had changed her voice. Every morning he inspected her for signs. But except for the week she was sick, he could see no difference at all. They had an old book that one of the missionaries' wives had given to Johnny Tulip's mother, *Truth, Fulfillment and Grace* it was called, a long and elegaic treatise on the joys of confinement, illustrated with tinted plates of ethereal prospective mothers wrapped in yards of filmy garments.

"Do you want a cigarette?" Laurel asked. The instrument panel had once been fancy and made out of wood. Now it was splintered and all the pieces stuck out at crazy angles. But the instruments still worked, and the lighter did too, dangling from wires so it could be swung to any position, pulled now by Laurel up to her mouth where she lit both cigarettes, handed one to Calvin.

"It's amazing," Laurel said. "I could tell you the world had ended and you wouldn't answer." The snow made it almost impossible to see the pavement. Since she had told him she was pregnant, they had existed in a new kind of truce, at least committed to go through whatever had been begun.

"I'd try," Calvin said. "I just wouldn't know what to say."

"Well. You could talk about the weather. It's been awfully cold lately. Or is it hot? I can never remember."

"Me neither," Calvin said. "I just live here." The feeling in his stomach had started again, opened up so quickly the last few peaceful weeks might never have existed. He had read an explanation of ulcers once, in a book that said they weren't necessary. At the top of the opening to the stomach, was a small narrow gland that squirted acid. The stomach was a bag filled with lining. When there was food inside as well, the acid was harmless. When there wasn't, it wore away the lining. After that it started to work on the walls of the stomach. Perhaps it only wanted to get out.

"You would have liked my parents," Laurel said. "My father was the strong, silent type. After the accident they discovered that his jaw had been wired shut for ten years." Now her voice was absolutely familiar, the same sharp tone she had when she talked about C.W., the doctor, salmon that were easily caught.

"You would have liked my parents too," Calvin said. "They were born at exactly the same time, on the same day, in the same year, both on trains. It was an amazing coincidence and it was reported in all the papers. They met at a dinner sponsored by the railroad."

"It must have been love at first sight."

"It was," Calvin said. "They went up to the observation car after dinner. They looked into each other's eyes."

"How romantic."

"The railroad supplied a gypsy to play love songs on the accordion. The next day he married them."

"What happened to the gypsy?"

"After the ceremony, he got off the train. It was a small prairie town with a railroad station. He invested his entire savings in nickels and persuaded the ticket-taker to feed the nickels, one at a time, into the locker where he stored his accordion and his tuxedo. Then he began to travel about the continent, hitch-hiking and hopping trains. He made his living as he always had, by entertaining people at weddings. He had two tricks: he could juggle oranges or he could eat the entire wedding cake. At small occasions he could do both at once, but he always charged extra. When the war came he was put out of business; no one could afford oranges and wedding cakes were filled with sand. He presented himself in Ottawa and offered his services as a spy. 'What can you do?' they asked him. In reply he ate the book of regulations. They sent him overseas. After the war he came back. He reclaimed his accordion. There were only four nickels left. He still tells his grandchildren the story of how he married my parents."

"That's nice," Laurel said. "Really." The tires hummed bald and uncertain through the snow. "You really have a talent for talking."

"In the east, we talk all night," Calvin said. For the first time since they had moved down to the cabin he remembered how he had first seen her, dangerous and sharp, a crazy woman running through the woods with her knife, her bottle, her taped-up rifle.

"My father and mother used to talk all the time," Laurel said.

196

"They should have had a telephone."

"Every Sunday night, before dinner, my father would plan the menu for the coming week. He couldn't cook but he knew how to eat. Of course he had to watch his weight."

"Or weight his watch," Calvin said. "People who talk a lot always think time flies."

"Jesus." She grabbed his arm and shook it, jerking the wheel, sending the truck skidding and fishtailing down the road. As it slid to a stop she was kneeling on the seat and laughing, her arms around him, pushing him back into the door.

The HOTEL sign was beginning to come into season, the green neon leaves running round the letters like hysterical reindeer, lighting up the snowy metal arm that held the sign out to the street. In the summer the front of the hotel had been lined with parked cars and the shouting and music escaping from the half-opened doors and windows had spilled out onto the street, swamping those who entered with incoherent noise, preparing them for worse. But now the street was almost empty. And the silence was only emphasized by the faint sounds of the piano, seeming from outside like an early Christmas toy that would be lucky to survive the month.

There was no one sitting at the registration counter of the hotel, only a buzzer to ring for service. The guest book was open; it was more than a week since anyone had signed it.

They crossed the lobby and stood at the entrance to the lounge. The door swung open and Mary Gail shot out, passed right by without even seeing them, ran down the hall to C.W.'s office. She fumbled at the lock and then closed herself inside. A few moments later she came out, much slower. She was carrying a small case of whiskey bottles.

The bandage was gone now. All the bruises had healed

and disappeared. There was only a small line where she had been cut. She smiled at Laurel, put the whiskey down and hugged her. Then she hugged Calvin too. It was so unexpected he didn't have time to move, only felt her pressing awkward and hot against him. But by the time he decided to put his arms around she had pushed back.

"I'm glad you came," Mary Gail said, more to Laurel than to Calvin it seemed. He saw they were holding hands, on the edge of giggling, like high school girls. Mary Gail was wearing a diamond ring.

"We thought we'd better get out," Calvin said. "Another week and the truck could be stuck for months." Mary Gail looked uncomprehendingly at him, and then at Laurel.

The piano had stopped. Two men pushed out from the lounge, wandered about the hall until they found the bathroom with the hat on the door. Calvin had his parka open. He was beginning to sweat. Laurel and Mary Gail were looking at each other vacantly. Laurel drew up the hand with the ring, inspected it closely.

"It's a nice ring," Calvin said. Mary Gail turned to him and she looked suddenly different than she ever had; her eyes large and brown, misted with liquid, she seemed to have emerged from some mythic country where there were no human beings, only large animals in pain, caught and waiting, waiting, like deer waiting to be shot.

"I better go back in," Mary Gail said. They pushed open the door, searched about the room for a table.

"Over there," Laurel said, pointing to a place where there were only two people: Johnny Tulip and an Indian woman whose face was amazingly wide, wider even than Johnny Tulip's, wide and pushed wider yet by a smile that stretched from one side to the other. She wore dark glasses that were somehow not incongruous, and a bright bandana tied through her hair, which was still thick and long, fell black and grey, fanned out wide across her shoulders. They were standing at the entrance, beside the bar, looking across the crowded room at Johnny Tulip and his mother. On the bar was a glass filled with yellow roses, more yellow roses from the mainland. Laurel took one and then held it carefully close, protecting it as they worked their way through. As she sat down, Laurel handed it to Johnny's mother. And she, in turn, wearing one of the innumerable suit tops that graced that household, placed it unerringly in her lapel, slipping the stem through the small slit that must have been meant for decorations, so only the flower showed, a round yellow rose.

Mary Gail appeared, set glasses of beer on the table. The glasses were filled to overflowing, the sides wet with foam. Again her arm brushed Calvin's, her skin electric on his, stopping momentarily at the tattoo, the anchor burned onto the back of his hand. Then she leaned over and said his name into her mother's ear, loud and distinct, as if she was deaf too.

The last time he had been thirsty. Now he was only nervous, drained two glasses quickly just to fill his stomach, give it something to do. Laurel's jeans were so faded and soft now, washed over and over through the summer and fall, he could feel her belly with her eyes. Their parkas looked absurdly bright, like twin flares. He was wearing a shirt that Laurel had given him. He felt confident, safe from everything in the extraordinary protection of Johnny's mother who had been facing him ever since Mary Gail's introduction, her smile so wide it seemed to include knowledge of anything possible, her eyes closed but benign behind the dark glasses, her head nodding minutely in his direction, not without approval.

Johnny's mother looked ancient but ageless, as if she

could endure like this forever, her skin so wrinkled and dried it had become something else, waves of dried brown cells held together by nothing but her own inexhaustible will. Calvin pushed his cigarettes across the table towards Johnny. He wanted for once to say something friendly and ordinary to him. He moved his legs and pulled his chair forward. There was a pressure against his thigh. He reached into his pocket and took out the red stone. It felt lukewarm and ordinary in his hand, something he had become accustomed to and didn't need any more. He leaned across the table, put it on top of the package.

"I found it on your birthday," Calvin said. "I should have given it to you then."

Johnny picked it up. It disappeared quickly into his big hand, stayed hidden while he extracted a cigarette from the package, was gone by the time the cigarette was lit and his hands were on the table again.

Tonight Johnny seemed even more tired and sick than usual. Whatever was wrong with him had now infiltrated all his movements, made them careless and rubbery, as if he had taken too many sleeping pills or his brain could no longer send out signals strong enough to tell his nerves what to do. He smoked slowly, didn't bother to check his coughs which shook him in his chair, gradually stringing together into a long staccato burst that finished only when he pounded his chest with his fist, hitting it so hard Calvin could hear the air being forced out.

Mary Gail passed the table again, more long glasses to add to the empties. Calvin drank slowly, the emergency already over and his stomach dulled and quiet. Johnny was hunched way over in his chair, resting his head on the table. His mother sat amazingly straight. She was turning her head slowly back and forth, as if scanning the room by radar. Her smile was impossibly wide and constant. There seemed to be a lot of coming and going from the entrance of the lounge, Indians and loggers gradually working their way in to fill the empty spaces.

The boy was standing beside the bar. He was wearing a new shirt and seemed to have melted into this island, smooth and sleek, his hair glossy and shining black, like a cat's. He saw Calvin watching him, raised his glass and nodded.

C.W., carrying an immense round tray of beer, stopped behind Johnny, put his hand on his shoulder. His beard had begun to fill out, made his face look even longer, his cheeks hollow and sunken. With his beard, his string tie, and his striped pants, he looked curiously formal, a man dressed up to make a speech. But he didn't say anything to Johnny, only touched him and moved on, the tray held high above his head, dipping at each table until finally it was only spotted with empty glasses and he had to work his way back towards the bar.

Johnny raised his head, looked at Calvin and Laurel as if noticing them for the first time and then, still not having spoken to them, pushed himself away from the table and stood up, wavering, supporting himself with his hands on the back of the chair. He coughed. "You shouldn't have come," he said, his voice harsh and broken. He coughed again, hammered his chest with his fist, and then turned away and started walking towards the piano.

They could have changed their minds at the road, walked back down the beach watching the moon try to occupy all the long sliding pools of water. Calvin took his parka off and hung it on the back of the chair. He pushed up the sleeves of his sweater, green wool, real wool, transformed by its life here, the wrists blackened and singed, the fibres clenched together by all the rainstorms it had been caught in. At home they would have been on the couch, would have undressed slowly, roasting their skins in the heat of the fire as if it was the sun. Laurel leaned forward, put her mouth to his ear, asked him to get her some scotch.

The boy was still at the bar, waved encouragement as Calvin wound towards him, slowly finding a path in the narrow empty spaces between the tables. The piano and the jukebox were both going. There was too much noise for anything to be heard separately. They had hired someone new to pour drinks and beer, a man Calvin had seen around the town but couldn't identify. Calvin ordered his drink and then leaned with his elbow on the bar, surveying the room. He was conscious of the boy being strangely close to him, edging closer as if there was something he wanted to say.

"How are you doing?" Calvin asked.

"I don't know," the boy said. "Jesus Christ, I might be drunk." He looped his arm around Calvin's neck. The boy was several inches shorter than Calvin and Calvin had to bend down to hear him above the noise in the bar.

"They say someone blew up the old mortuary poles from the old village," the boy said. "Mary Gail told me her father's buried down there."

"When?"

"This afternoon," the boy said. The lounge was packed. All the tourists and government men were gone now, but the lounge was more crowded than when Calvin had come to the island, more crowded than he had ever seen it. The centre tables were filled with loggers. Perhaps one of them had been the one to dynamite the poles. Or perhaps it had been C.W. himself, or even the boy. The tables of the loggers were covered with glasses of beer. And the tables of Indians too, all the tables along the wall, surrounding the loggers not with hostility or anger, but only a curious kind of waiting.

"They shouldn't have done it," the boy said. Calvin nodded. Laurel had taken him to see the poles once. Now there would be nothing left of them at all, only dust, burnt wood, and tiny fragments of bone scattered equally about the clearing.

C.W. and Mary Gail were both serving beer, expertly threading their way between the tables with full trays, too busy to talk or make jokes. But when Mary Gail passed by the stage Johnny Tulip leaned over and whispered to her. Calvin saw Mary Gail try to move away, saw C.W. stop and watch too. Johnny grabbed her arm and kept talking to her. All the Indians in the bar stood up, raised their glasses together. Something was shouted but Calvin couldn't understand the words. He looked around for Laurel. She was still sitting at their table, now talking with Johnny Tulip's mother. The rose that Laurel had given her was pinned to her dress, yellow and delicate, and her smile had grown from what it had been to a huge cupped grin that still went right across her face.

Mrs. Harry Jones, Johnny Tulip's mother, smiled hugely all the way around the room. C.W. came and stood beside her, replaced her empty glass. As he set the new one on the table she swept it off, sending it flying onto the floor. Her smile remained fixed on her face.

"She still needs a drink," Laurel said.

C.W. looked up towards the piano. Johnny had stopped playing. Mary Gail was standing beside Johnny, holding a tray of bottles.

"Maybe you don't want any more," C.W. said.

She laughed. She stood up. She was fat and short. She placed her hand flat against C.W.'s chest. Then she took a glass from his tray and sat down. She laughed again showing teeth of every variety, some white and whole, some broken, one tipped with gold, some dark and decayed.

Johnny Tulip had stopped playing the piano but the jukebox was still on, the bass thudding through the room, shaking the floor.

"It was a mistake," C.W. said. "I'm sorry."

"Screw you," Johnny Tulip's mother said. Her voice was tough and sharp, cut easily through the noise of the lounge.

C.W. shrugged. "I'm sorry," he said. He sat down too, in between Laurel and Johnny Tulip's mother. The record on the jukebox was over. An Indian sat on top of it, swinging his heels against its face. Calvin's drink was pushed across the counter to him. He started to reach in his pocket but the boy was quicker, slapping down a twenty dollar bill, crisp and new, folded neatly in half. The tables of loggers were quiet and tense. Glasses were being raised and emptied. Calvin began working his way back towards his table. The boy stuck with him, his hand on his shoulder, curiously weightless.

"It was someone new," C.W. said. "He didn't know what he was doing."

"Screw you," Johnny Tulip's mother said again. She pushed the tray off the table. The glasses broke in a long cascade, a long glass cough.

The sound of breaking glass froze the room. Only Calvin and the boy were still moving, walking, Johnny saw, down the narrow alley that would lead them to his mother's table, the crazy rhythms of the boy's drunken walk jumping and collapsing through his blood, as the piano keys once had, jumping through Johnny Tulip's blood and now through everyone in that crowded bar so each person began to make all those small shifts and adjustments they would need. And with each tiny motion of each person Johnny Tulip could feel the boundaries of his skin collapsing, his nervous system reaching out to embrace the whole room. Standing with his mother in the centre, pushing out and testing with Laurel, pushing C.W. further, daring him to live out this moment which had now snared them all, was slowly drawing them to their feet, the loggers who had filtered into town over the past few weeks, the Indians who surrounded them now in the lounge as in their dreams, Laurel Hobson, as bold and fixed as Victoria had been. And while his mother waited in the centre, calm and squat in this now solid waiting forest of human flesh, the boy and Calvin still converged towards her, Calvin leading, the boy with one arm draped over him.

"I guess I'll get some more beer," C.W. said. "I'm sorry." Turned and started to run out of the room, down the narrow alley between the loggers and the Indians. As quick as he moved the boy moved too, tugged as if by a string. After him, Calvin. And finally Johnny, for the first time since Victoria's death spread out this way, could feel everything that moved through him. Pushed up from the piano, rocked back and then jumped forward off the stage and onto the floor of the lounge, the heels of his boots smashing into the wood, jolting him even more alive, his skeleton sprung taut and lithe so he could feel his bones knit close and quick together, as they once had been, close and quick so his mind moved easily through them, the whole room registered in his every movement as he slid through it, finally reached the door of the lounge to see C.W. struggling with the boy in his office, Calvin coming up behind him, reaching over the boy.

"He's mine," Johnny wanted to shout, but knew he wasn't, that this had nothing more to do with him. But still his own momentum carried him down the hall. And now he could see that the boy and C.W. were fighting over a rifle that C.W. now swung towards the boy, hitting him on the side of the head, knocking him to the floor.

And Calvin, almost upon them now, was already reaching

over the boy to grab at C.W. who was swinging the rifle towards him. But the boy was quickest of all, was up on his feet again instantly, his shoulder knocking Calvin's arm aside, one quick hand wrapped into C.W.'s long string tie, the other pushed out to meet the rifle.

The explosion took Calvin by surprise, so loud and unexpected it was truly the first noise he had heard in the months since Laurel Hobson shot the deer. And in the moment it took him to start moving again Calvin saw the boy's hand splay out, expand so suddenly and quickly he thought it had been blow off.

Even as he reached them he only began to see what was happening, that the boy's hair was thick with blood, that his whole body had been pushed back by the impact but now moved forward once more, as if by recoil, his hand closing now like a night flower, sinking in C.W. and bending him double.

Calvin ran right into the boy, pushing him further into C.W. as he himself reached out for C.W.'s throat, the boy's hand still there, knotted loosely into the tie. His mind seemed to hardly exist now, all but one part concentrating on the problem of who was dead and who was alive, that remaining part uncertain and aware of the crowd behind him, waiting and neutral, only whites fighting in this office. And in the instant of this new hesitation there was the second explosion, the sound oddly muffled at first, but staying with him, growing right into his body and opening it up, splitting across all his nerves and then emerging finally at his hip, bursting out from that point where the bone had been touched; and the hesitation was sealed into him now, a hot bar pressed against his side, welding his leg and his hip and his ribs into one long moment that pressed him against the falling boy, the boy's blood following the bullet's path into him, cushioning the long slow fall. And even as he fell, he twisted, holding onto the boy as the boy held dead but unyielding to C.W.'s tie, twisted and saw Johnny Tulip come crashing over them like a huge blind shadow, smashing into C.W. and hiding the rifle as it went off the third and final time, the sound muffled and broken.

Fourteen

They buried the boy in the cemetery behind the clinic. At the last moment the doctor found space for one more grave. They had stayed up all night watching him die and they put him in the earth the next morning, not even bothering to embalm him. The police had waited with them. Then drove C.W.'s body down to the airport, in his own hearse, to be taken to Montana.

Even while the doctor had been trying to save the boy, his wife knew it was hopeless. "It had to happen," she said to Laurel, flatly, her lips pursed together in final judgment.

Calvin got out of bed for the funeral. His hip was padded with bandages, bulged so far they had to get him a pair of bigger pants. The doctor supplied those, and a thick rubber-tipped cane. Calvin stood over the grave, leaning on his cane and on Laurel, who stood beside him, her arm through his.

They laid the boy's coffin in the earth, Johnny Tulip at one end and the doctor at the other. Then the doctor, still wearing his white coat, stained now with blood and disinfectant, wrinkled from the days and nights since the shooting, positioned himself at the front of the grave and bowed his head. "Earth to earth, dust to dust," he said loudly. He looked around. "May his soul rest in peace," he added. He took the shovel from the small mound of earth they had dug out and threw the first of it back onto the plain cedar coffin. After a while he handed the shovel to Johnny Tulip and Johnny, untouched by the collision with C.W., finished digging the boy's grave, working slowly and methodically.

It was a grey day but not cold or raining. Calvin's side still felt open and warm. But though he checked it constantly there was no new blood on the bandage. And when he walked it was stiff but it didn't hurt as badly as it might have. He stayed with Laurel at the grave after the others had left. The earth was mounded, wet black earth laced with sand. Soon it would dissolve this coffin, open it and take back its own. Somewhere in him he still had the boy's blood, mixed with his own. The wound had closed quickly, not serious the doctor had said, the bullet already slowed by what it had passed through.

"I never liked him," Laurel said. "I guess he was all right."

"I hope so."

"Well," Laurel said. "I feel stupid standing here." She looked up at Calvin and then they both turned back to the grave. A few needles had already blown across the earth. He moved his arm along her back. Her shoulder was small and warm in his hand, like a bird's wing, delicate and precise, propelled through space by the movement of small bones. She faced him, slid her arms into his open parka, pushed herself against his chest. Her hair smelled of woodsmoke and the sea. He felt her crying and it made him cry too, his throat tight and painful at first, and then releasing, with the flow of his tears, unsure if he was crying for the boy, himself, or the wet winter that still lay ahead.

When they went back inside, the doctor and Johnny Tulip were waiting for them. The doctor had put his jeans into a shopping bag, and added a supply of bandages and dressings.

"Of course you shouldn't leave," he said to Calvin, handing him the bag and then clasping his hands together. He cracked his knuckles, then stopped himself, pulled his hands apart and put them in the pockets of his white coat. He smiled and looked away. "We don't have any more graves," he said. His wife was sitting behind the reception desk, reading a paperback book. "So we can't have any more dying here," the doctor concluded. He began walking towards the door, finished with talking for the day.

Calvin adjusted himself carefully in the truck, moving his hip well away from the door before he closed it. Through the mirror he could see the doctor framed on the steps, looking tiny and white, waving briefly, a photograph taken from too great a distance. He drove carefully, his foot unsure and weak on the clutch. As always the streets were empty and the town seemed deserted. In front of the hotel a police car was parked, ferried over from the mainland. No one had remembered to turn off the sign and the flashing letters and leaves were strangely visible, pulsing through the mist that had now begun to drift over the town. Soon it would rain and the snow would be gone again.

As always the streets were empty and the town seemed deserted. The aluminum siding of the management houses shone white and pink through the rain. But when they got to the old village, the houses seemed to have faded, looked as grey and wispy as the mist which stretched in a thick porous blanket down to the cove where they could see it squatting stolidly over the water like a dark giant mushroom.

They stopped at Johnny Tulip's house and Laurel had to come around to the driver's side, help Calvin down from the truck. He noticed for the first time that beside Johnny Tulip's house was an ancient rusted car. It stood at a strange angle, supported by an old stump. Its front wheels leaned against it. Long grass grew up on all sides, through the rusted out holes in the fenders, up from underneath in long green fingers.

The house was as quiet as the street. Mary Gail was sitting alone at the kitchen table, reading a magazine. She stood up as they came banging in the door, pushed the kettle over the fire. Her hair had just been washed; it hung close to her head, damp and stringy.

"I should have gone," she said. "I knew he wouldn't care." She found some cups in the sink, and held them up to the tap. Water splashed everywhere, out of the cups onto the counter and the floor. When she was finished she set them on the table, wet and stained.

Calvin eased himself down carefully, holding the table for support. It was best with his leg straight out, his heel on the floor. His hip was warm and throbbing. The doctor's pants were too short for him, rode up past his socks to his shins. They were old khaki pants with wide cuffs, and a waist so roomy that even with his bandages it had bunched up under the belt. He adjusted his leg. He slid his hand into the pants, felt the bandage for blood. It was warm but dry. The doctor had sewn everything closed, twenty stitches, he had said, inside and out. In the old days they would have let him bleed, applied leeches and waited for him to die. They could have opened the clinic window for him, given him a bow and arrow to choose his grave.

"Let's see," Mary Gail said. She pulled up his sweater. His side was swollen and red, tender where she touched it. She spread her fingers along the edge of the bandage and then pushed, the pressure sudden and sharp, a knife drawn through the very centre of the wound, cutting whatever it was that had been making it numb and stiff, his whole side flooded with pain, shooting from his leg to his shoulder as some mysterious circulation was restored.

"That's better," she said. She poured the boiling water from the kettle into the teapot. There was a cough from the next room.

"We should go in there," Johnny said, nodding towards the living-room. Johnny and Mary Gail went in first, carrying the tea and the cups. Calvin stood up slowly, his side still painful and buzzing.

The curtains were drawn and even by comparison with the kitchen and the grey outside, this room was so dark Calvin could barely see, was aware of nothing but a jumble of furniture and cartons. Gradually objects began to resolve. There was a staircase on the far side of the room, its bannister slung with clothes of every description. In the centre of the room, on the floor, was an ancient Persian rug, so thick with dust and age that its colours and patterns had run into each other, left now only a memory of tassels and brocades, archways moving towards an unusual centre, a yellow sun that exploded out in sharp geometric spikes.

The darkened window faced out onto the verandah. Under it was an old and battered couch. Opposite the couch Johnny Tulip's mother was sitting, almost invisible at the back of the room, rocking slowly in a wicker chair. On one side of her was an old loom, covered with skeins of wool that were themselves layered by dust and cobwebs. On the other, backed into the wall, was a glass bookcase that rose from floor to ceiling, was filled with what seemed to be the remains of an indefinite number of china services.

She stood up as Laurel and Calvin came into the room. She was wearing her sunglasses still, but had nothing over her head. Her hair seemed bushy and electric, stood out from her head and flowed down over her shoulders in a great rush of silver and black. "Well," she said. She held out her hand to Laurel. "You finally got away." Even in this quiet house her voice was flat and dry, cut through the darkness and the dust.

212

Then she turned to Calvin, grasped his wrist with her hand. She moved with uncanny agility. In the confusion of the dark she had seemed to stand up effortlessly, carried by a current. And as her fingers closed around his arm Calvin thought he could hear a vague rustling, the surface of her skin crackling like parchment. Her face did not seem the face of a young person turned old but had its own complete character, the cells reborn into this final incarnation.

"He drove us back," Johnny said.

"That was very kind." She still held onto Calvin's arm, her fingers insistent and hard, the flesh transparent to the touch now, her bones against his, dry and old.

"We should have tea," Johnny said. He had set the pot down on the low circular table that separated his mother from the rest of the room, a beautifully polished table that Harry Jones had made for her, the hand-split cedar boards joined together and polished.

"It's a nice table," Calvin said. He had never seen cedar worked like this, the grain dark and luminous. On the table were two long grey needles, pierced through some brightly coloured wool.

"My husband made it for me." She let go Calvin's arm and sat back down in her chair. Mary Gail spread the cups out beside the pot, a long straight row that went right across the table.

"My husband's dead."

"I'm sorry," Calvin said.

Johnny's mother laughed harshly. She turned to Laurel. "He says he's sorry."

"It's true," Laurel said. "He wouldn't say it if he didn't mean it."

Johnny Tulip's mother clasped her hands and rocked in her wicker chair. Johnny lifted the lid of the teapot, smelled the steam. There were more wicker chairs. They pulled them up and sat around the table. Calvin was getting used to the light of this room. He could see the birds enamelled on the side of the teapot, the two yellow canaries that tipped as Johnny poured the tea.

"My husband was strong. You see that car outside? My husband lifted that car into the air with his hands. He held it up while his lazy son put the log in place."

"I was trying to help," Johnny said.

"Trying to help," his mother mimicked. "If God told you to go to the bathroom you'd probably piss in your pants."

The tea spilled, steaming onto the polished smooth cedar.

In the kitchen Laurel found the cloth, warm and stiff from hanging near the stove. She took it into the living-room and spread it carefully on the table, a sour square sail that she dragged around the edges. Then Johnny finished pouring the tea, the yellow canaries bending with each remaining cup.

"You see? He can't do anything." She had taken off her glasses. The lids of her eyes quivered in the dark room. Laurel pushed her chair closer to Calvin, reached into his coat pocket for the cigarettes.

Johnny's mother sipped at her tea. "My husband was an elegant man," she said. Her voice was hard and authoritative. She might have been giving a lecture. "He used to dance," she said. "We used to go out on the beach and he would dance for me."

"It's true," Mary Gail said.

"Yes," Johnny said. His words were barely audible, caught in his throat. He coughed. Then he went into the kitchen and coughed again. There was the sound of the stove being opened and then slammed closed. Johnny came back into the room. He was carrying the kettle. He stood over the polished wooden table. With one hand he lifted the lid of the pot; with the other he carefully brought the kettle forward, added the new water.

"You see? You can do anything if you try."

Laurel felt something jump in her stomach. Soon it would be time to go home. The tide was low now, it would be easy to walk up the beach. The cabin would be cold and damp. They would start a fire, burn the wetness out. Calvin would sleep on his back to protect his hip. It would give him bad dreams and he would be restless in the night. They would have to make love carefully. The doctor hadn't said anything about it. She had dozed on the bed beside Calvin while they were trying to save the boy. Sometimes she went into the room next door, to see how they were doing. The boy had been unconscious, a bottle of plasma dripping into his arm. They were trying to save him, the doctor had said. Really, she knew better; like the doctor's wife she knew they were only waiting. At the end only Laurel had been there. The boy had opened his eyes, recognized her, and closed them again.

"My husband always carried a handkerchief," Johnny's mother said. She would probably outlive him. And right after his funeral she would start to lie about him. Soon he would be a concert pianist. Soon he would die in a plane crash over Europe.

"When my husband danced, the whole world stopped." She leaned forward and held her hand over the table. She moved it across, slowly, a few inches off the surface. When it was above the cigarettes it stopped, hovered briefly, and then descended, fingers arched like a hawk. Her eyelids quivered. Unerringly she leaned forward to meet the match that Johnny held out for her.

Calvin had already finished his tea, was taking another cup. His hand shook nervously. "It's all right," Johnny said. "She has the second sight." He tried to laugh but it got tangled in his throat, turned into more coughs. His

215

mother's face was so huge and so wide, that beside her Johnny looked only normal, his giant features almost immature, still aging and gathering strength, still separate from each other, all the scars and bumps and once-broken bones individually visible, not yet melted together into one vast and unified dark map. Johnny's mother leaning forward now towards Laurel and making it her responsibility to push the room from this moment to the next, waiting, and then putting out her hand for Laurel's, her cigarette over at the side of her wide mouth.

"I used to read tea leaves," the old woman said. "Now I can only read palms." But she didn't even trace the lines with her fingers, only rested her palm on top of Laurel's palm, cool and liquid, her ancient skin impossibly soft.

Laurel looked at Mary Gail, and then back at the old woman, back and forth again. Mary Gail's eyes were closed and she was slouched in her chair. Sweat stood out on her forehead in tiny beaded rows. The old woman's palm moved slightly, the skin soft and pliable, soft as Mary Gail's, grasped her hand as if to swallow it, as if to pull Laurel to her.

"This is the way it has to be," the old woman said. Mary Gail's skin had been liquid too, the scent from her body this faded and used.

The rain must have started again. It hummed against the windows and the roof, reminding her of outboard motors, the totem pole that sat above the cove. When she had stood up from Mary Gail's bed and looked out the window, the pole had seemed transformed, as if deep within itself, half-rotted and scarred by weather and random knives, it was secretly alive. In the spring they would get a boat and explore the coast of this island, go to the isolated inlets and bays where the old villages used to be, their long log houses and old fire-pits still visible in their remains, strange piles of bones, the bleached white showing through

216

moss and grass, logs with long rows of birds floating slowly off the beach, spirit birds, they used to say, the souls of the ancestors watching over their graves.

Calvin's shoulder slid by hers as he reached for his tea, the signal of his presence like a magnet, pulling her away, dividing her into zones. The current between Calvin and the old woman flowed through her body. Her hand was burning and painful in the old woman's grasp, which was now locked tight; their bones fused together, the old woman's delicate and hollow, fragile shells concealed in flesh and cloth.

Her vast dark face was frozen and still. She was so close Laurel could see the thousands of tiny cross-hatched wrinkles spread in waves through her skin.

"My husband was strong, he could hold up a tree."

"A dead man can hold up a forest," Johnny said. His mother's wide mouth jerked into a smile, a sudden meaningless movement that quickly closed. She released Laurel's hand, sank back into her chair. Her cigarette was still buried in the corners of her lips. She wrapped her fingers around it, pulled it out carefully, as if it might have put down roots.

William-and-Mary wouldn't have known what to say about each other if one had died first, would have had to spend hours staring at old photographs, reconstructing bits and pieces to prove that someone had been alive. Laurel looked hopelessly around the room to see if there might be a drink. Soon it would be time to go home. She checked the back of her chair, feeling for her coat. The nylon scratched. along her nails, a high uncomfortable noise. It would stay raining all evening and the rain and the ocean spray would soak them through. It would be good to get home wet, the cabin cold and wet too, so they would have to start a fire to dry out everything. And by the time they were warm, by the time they had eaten and cleaned the dishes, the cabin would smell of smoke and dry cotton, and they would sleep to the sound of rain and burning wood.

Johnny's mother took the knitting from the table her husband had made her. With her fingers she counted the stitches, then, her mouth moving with them, began clicking the needles together. Laurel looked down at Calvin's cup. It was almost full, the surface oily and glazed. Calvin reached for his cane, pushed back his chair.

"Thank you for the tea," he said.

"You say so."

"Me too," Laurel said. "Really." She put on her coat and felt in her pocket for her wallet. Johnny's mother had set down her knitting. She was facing Laurel.

"My husband was so strong," she said. "Johnny was always afraid of him."

"He was too fat," Johnny said.

"Please."

"His gut hung out over his belt." Johnny opened his jacket, looked at his own stomach. He sucked it in and slapped it sharply. "Soon I'll be fat like him," Johnny said.

"You shouldn't say that." The old woman seemed suddenly helpless and blind, trapped in this room, behind her husband's cedar table.

In the spring they would explore the coast, live on mussels and clams, make salads of wild peas and plantain. "I'll just finish," Laurel said. She pulled at Calvin's arm. Her cup was already empty, sat lightly on the smooth shining wood.

"That's better," the old woman said. "You can't let them drag you around." She laughed. "Harry was too fat to drag anything."

Laurel looked across at Johnny. His long broken fingers were twisted together, white with pressure. In Vancouver she lay on the beach and he lay beside her, his breath on her, his breath on her face like an ancient wind, filled with dreams and old songs that played through her blood like half-heard voices, like the ragged songs he pounded out on the piano. The lounge would be closed for a couple of months and then someone else from the city would buy the hotel. By summer it would be open again. In the dream the band had marched loudly up the hill, stood in the centre of the open space, their playing bold and aggressive, every note blindly searching for the finale. Through the sand and the pounding of the waves she had been able to feel his heart, pumping so strong it shook the whole beach, swallowing the energy of the waves and beating each one out in perfect rhythm, his spirit taut and strong as a drumskin, strong now too, hovering untouched in the centre of his body, a visitor poised for flight.

"Well," Laurel said. She stood up.

The old woman rose too, facing her. She reached out and took Laurel's hand. Her eyelids quivered. "You have a good future," the old woman said. She laughed harshly. She opened her eyes. In each socket was a luminous wooden eyeball, the grain streaked and polished.